THE TRAITORS

Also by Leo Kessler

THE IRON FIST

In the *Wotan/Panzer* Series

SS PANZER BATTALION
DEATH'S HEAD
CLAWS OF STEEL
GUNS AT CASSINO
THE DEVIL'S SHIELD
HAMMER OF THE GODS
FORCED MARCH
BLOOD AND ICE
THE SAND PANTHERS

In the *Black Cossacks* Series

THE BLACK COSSACKS
THE BLACK COSSACKS 2: SABRES OF THE REICH
THE BLACK COSSACKS 3: MOUNTAIN OF SKULLS

In the *Stormtroop* Series

STORMTROOP

Leo Kessler

The Traitors

Futura Publications Limited
A Futura Book

A Futura Book

First published in Great Britain by
Futura Publications Limited in 1977

ISBN 0 8600 7597 4

Printed in Great Britain by
Hazell Watson & Viney Ltd
Aylesbury, Bucks

Futura Publications Limited
110 Warner Road
Camberwell, London SE5

'The Bolsheviks are our superiors in only one field – espionage'

Adolf Hitler

'In the high ranges of Secret Service work, the actual facts in many cases were in every respect equal to the most fantastic inventions of romance and melodrama. Tangle within tangle, plot and counter-plot, ruse and treachery, cross and double-cross, true agent, false agent, double agent, gold and steel, the bomb, the dagger, and the firing party, were interwoven in many a texture so intricate as to be incredible and yet true. The Chief and the High Officers of the Secret Service revelled in these subterranean labyrinths and pursued their task with cold and silent passion.'

Winston Churchill.

A BRIEF GLOSSARY OF TERMS

Pianist – radio operator.

Music Box – transmitter.

Orchestra – spy ring.

Conductor – local head of spy ring.

Resident or *Rezident* – Head of Russian Intelligence in any particular country. A *resident* can be both *legal* (i.e. working under diplomatic cover) or *illegal* (i.e. without any official cover, that is a spy).

Director – Head of Soviet Intelligence at the Moscow *Centre*, i.e. HQ.

Abwehr – German Intelligence.

Tirpitzufer – Berlin HQ of *Abwehr*.

Prinzalbrechtstrasse – Berlin HQ of *Gestapo* (German Secret Police).

Funkabwehr – German radio detection service.

Shoemaker – Forger.

Treff – clandestine meeting place.

'C' – Head of the British Secret Intelligence Service (SIS).

Old Firm – British Intelligence.

ONE: DEATH OF A PIANIST

MEMO DATED APRIL 1st, 1941 (Confidential)
FROM 'C' TO LT. COMMANDER RIX

Dear Rix,

I am sending you a 'body' down to Exmouth in a few days. Please ensure that he doesn't miss the boat. I am sending you his orders by special courier. Will you take it upon yourself to see that the 'body' understands each point completely?

Yours Aye
C

SIGNAL.

00142. TOP SECRET

FROM. SIS to BOATS.

SUBJECT. OPERATIONAL ORDERS FOR CAPT. WILLIAM WILY (R.A.C. 1084, 175)

1. Wily will be transported from harbour at high tide April 14th, 1941.
2. He will be attached to French Resistance with effect time-of-arrival.
3. Wily's cover biography, ID, personal documents, ration card will be forwarded by hand. A weapon will not be supplied.

CHAPTER ONE

Now it was curfew.

The blacked-out streets of the Belgian capital were empty. The civilians were safely tucked away for the night behind the shuttered windows of their nineteenth-century houses, listening to their radios or already sleeping, one more grey day of total war behind them. The only sound was the metallic clatter and shudder of the shunting trains across at the Laeken railway yard.

Captain Peipe, the empty sleeve of his grey tunic tucked neatly into his pistol-belt, looked down the cobbled slope of the Rue de Atrebas, and noted with approval that his men were beginning to take up their positions now, their sock-covered boots almost noiseless. He nodded his silent approval. Everything was going according to plan.

He glanced at the green-glowing dial of his wristwatch. Nearly midnight. Five minutes to go to zero hour. Soon he would find the pianist they had been looking for every damn night for the last three months. Then he might perhaps get a good night's sleep for a change.

The long hunt for the pianist had begun in the spring of 1941. Peipe had just been posted to the *Abwehr's* counter-espionage office in Brussels after the loss of his arm in the French campaign. 'Wine, women and song, you lucky dog,' his comrades in Mainz Military Hospital had commented enviously when he had told them he was being sent to the Belgian capital. 'You always land on your feet, One-Flipper. It'll be roses all the way.'

They had been gravely wrong. Almost immediately, the *Abwehr's* listening post at Kranz had reported that an illegal pianist was operating somewhere in the Belgium–Northern France area. 'God in Heaven,' he had cursed when he had received the signal and Canaris's* order to find the pianist. 'They might as well say that the bastard is operating in Patagonia!'

All the same, he had set about finding the pianist, using all that energy and skill which had made him such a feared public prosecutor in Berlin in the old days before he had decided that he would be safer from the Nazis in the *Wehrmacht* than in the National Socialist Justice Department.

Although he was completely new to intelligence work, he had reasoned that although his quarry was a hunted animal, he had not an animal's mobility; for as a rule a pianist always transmitted from the same spot. All the same, hidden in a large city, the pianist enjoyed the same cover as a wild animal located deep in a thick forest. First, Peipe told himself, he would have to find the particular city from which the unknown pianist operated.

He had called in the *Luftwaffe* radio detection experts. Within a month they had found the pianist's hiding place. It was Brussels; his own station! Now the really hard work had begun. Armed with a street map of Brussels, a pair of celluloid discs, with markings graduated from zero to three hundred and sixty degrees, and with a silken thread attached to each disc, Captain Peipe and his *Luftwaffe* radio experts had commenced

* Admiral Canaris, head of the *Abwehr*, the German Intelligence Service.

the wearisome process of trying to locate the pianist's hideout.

By a stroke of luck the experts had managed to get their silken threads to intersect over the Brussels suburb of Laeken. The pianist was operating from that grubby, working-class area.

Thereafter the real hard slog had begun. Armed with the heavy suitcase-like mobile detectors, Piepe and his experts had tramped through the blacked-out streets night after night, trying to discover the particular house in which the pianist was using his music box.

Then the unknown pianist seemed to scent that the hunt was on. He had changed his hiding-place in Laeken several times. Twice Peipe had come across lookouts who had fled into the silent darkness as soon as they had spotted the 'suitcase men'. The 'concerts' had become much shorter, too.

Peipe had countered by having the *Luftwaffe* experts jam the pianist's concerts so that he would have to stay on the air longer, wasting precious minutes.

The pianist had responded to the challenge by changing his wavelength and call-signs repeatedly. Apparently he had several music boxes at his disposal, and he changed from one to another three or four times a week. Peipe could almost sense the unknown pianist's agonised suspense as he felt the trap slowly but surely begin to close in on him, and he could not help but admire the man's bravery and nerve.

By the end of the tenth week of the hunt, Peipe had narrowed down the area from which the pianist was transmitting to several streets near Laeken's shunting yard. Time after time he had sprung midnight raids on individual houses, while the pianist was working. By throwing the main switches, one by one, and checking whether the music box stopped playing, he could tell whether the pianist was on the premises or not.

It had been a silent and stealthy hunt, with no echoing horns, no excited hunters. All the same it was going to end like any hunt for fox or stag: with the killing of the quarry. And that moment was at hand – the pianist was operating this night from 101 Rue d'Atrebas.

Captain Peipe raised his whistle to his lips, paused and then blew hard. The men of the Secret Field Police sprang from their hiding places. A hard shoulder crashed against the door of Number 101. There was a cry of alarm. A knife of yellow light slashed the darkness as the door opened. Peipe ran forward. Inside the house someone fired his pistol, once, twice, three times. To Peipe in the entrance hall, the reports sounded like small bombs going off. He halted, chest heaving from the effort of running, and looked round. An elderly man lay writhing on the floor, grabbing for his bloody belly. Next to him a middle-aged woman, her skirt thrown up to reveal her patched white underwear, was crouched, screaming with the pain of her wound.

'No more shooting!' Peipe yelled. 'I want the pianist alive!'

'*Jawohl, Herr Hauptmann*,' the burly police sergeant, who had done the shooting, cried.

While the other policemen started to spread out to search the ground floor, Peipe and the sergeant tumbled up the dingy staircase, heavy with the smell of unwashed bodies and the raw, heavily-spiced mincemeat which the Belgians loved to eat. At the landing they hesitated, wondering which direction to take. There were closed doors everywhere.

'Let's check them out from left to right.' Peipe decided.

The police sergeant nodded his agreement. He slammed his big boot against the first door. It flew open. The room was empty save for a makeshift bed and a can full of urine.

'Belgie pigs!' the sergeant snorted in disgust. 'Filthy habits they have.'

'Come on,' Peipe ordered. 'We've no time to waste on Belgian sanitary habits.'

They opened the next door. Peipe saw the man cowering there and reacted instinctively like the combat soldier he had once been before his arm was shot away at Sedan. He flung himself to one side and grabbed for his pistol. The sergeant wasn't so quick. The civilian fired, and at that close range, the bullet which thwacked into the sergeant's belly lifted him clean off his feet and slammed him against the wall. Peipe didn't hesitate. As the sergeant slithered down the wall, dragging a trail of blood behind him, Peipe fired. The civilian smashed into the black-out curtains, his spectacles sliding absurdly from his suddenly agonised face. He was dead.

'Damn and blast!' Peipe cursed, and lowered his pistol. He flung a look at the sergeant. He lay slumped in a heap, his false teeth bulging out of his mouth. He was unconscious, his breath coming in short, harsh gasps. He was obviously seriously wounded.

'*Sanitäter*,' Peipe cried at the top of his voice. 'Up here – *at the double*!'

Peipe forgot the sergeant. He would have to take his chance like every other serviceman. Pistol still clasped warily in his hand, Peipe took stock of the room.

There were documents and papers everywhere. Even a cursory glance told him that most of the documents were German, which seemed strange. But he had no time for them. His eyes were fixed on the transmitter on the table next to the dead civilian. He touched it. It was still warm. It had been in use until a few moments before. Peipe looked at the jacket hanging over the back of the chair next to the table and then at the pair of shoes at its foot. The pianist had obviously felt secure enough this night to make himself comfortable. And now he was dead.

Peipe grunted to himself, and placing his pistol on the table, picked up the first document. It gave detailed figures of last month's production of the Mark IV tank, broken down by area. Peipe whistled softly.

Behind him the medical orderly was beginning to open the unconscious sergeant's tunic to get at the stomach wound. Peipe took up another document. Again it was in German and again it contained top-secret information about the proposed *Wehrmacht* offensive against Moscow, complete with statistics, equipment to be used, numbers of aircraft involved, even the names of the commanders of the divisions to be employed.

Peipe looked angrily at the dead civilian. Where in three devils' names had the shabby civilian obtained information of that quality? Who in Germany was supplying him with that kind of material? The traitor or spy must be right at the top. Otherwise he would not have been able to get that kind of information. God, if the civilian were only able to talk!

Behind him the sergeant groaned miserably as the orderly, his fingers red with blood, started to plug the gaping wound in the fat greasy belly.

'Shut up!' Peipe said unfeelingly. 'I can't even think with you making that kind of racket. Orderly, give him a—'

Peipe broke off suddenly and stared at the dead civilian's feet. The man still had his shabby shoes on. But the pianist had been in his stockinged feet. The dead man *wasn't* the pianist after all!

Peipe glanced round the room, looking for a hiding place. There wasn't one. The room was bare; there wasn't even a cupboard. He looked upwards. Above him, a small dormer window was half open. The pianist had escaped onto the roof!

He knew it instinctively. He sprang on to the table and poked his head through the window.

Scarlet flame stabbed the inky darkness. A bullet howled off a tile only half a metre away from his head. Peipe ducked hurriedly. From down below in the street, someone shouted, 'Look out! The bastard's hidden by the chimney!'

Peipe dropped to the floor and grabbed his pistol. He clattered down the stairs. His men had taken cover in the street and were preparing to fire. 'Don't fire!' Peipe yelled urgently. 'I want him alive. *Don't fire!*'

The words were drowned by the excited burst of automatic fire from the roof. The bullets struck up a trail of fiery blue sparks on the cobbles to their front.

Then the pianist was up and running crazily along the steeply-sloping roof. There was the crash of breaking glass. A woman screamed, as if woken suddenly from a deep sleep.

'He's making a bolt for it!' Peipe cried. 'After him, lads!'

The police needed no urging. They broke from their cover and doubled down the street. They burst into the house from which the cry had come. Excited, frightened Belgians in their underclothes or shabby dressing-gowns were standing everywhere on the gas-lit landings. A fat woman with pendulous breasts bulging unappetizingly through her nightgown, her hair in paper curlers, was jabbering in Flemish.

'Where is he?' Peipe interjected in French.

'Gone . . . gone,' she cried.

'Spread out,' Peipe commanded. 'He must be in the house somewhere. At the double, lads. He mustn't get away this time. This one's a really big fish. There'll be a three-day pass to Paris for the man who captures him!'

Swiftly the police combed the house from top to bottom. There was no sign of the pianist. Peipe began to fear the worst. Then there was an excited cry from the cellar. Peipe clattered down the dark stone steps into the dimly-lit cellar, stinking of winter potatoes and turnips. A grinning *Obergefreiter* had his rifle levelled at a hard-featured man in his early forties, who was kneeling on the floor next to an old tin bath.

'Funny time to want to have a bath, sir,' the corporal said, obviously pleased with himself and the prospect of three days' leave in Paris. 'And he didn't have any water in it anyway.'

Peipe ignored the soldier. Instead he stepped forward and grabbed the civilian's right hand. He held it up to the dim light and stared hard at the man's index finger. It was still red and dented with the effort of tapping the morse key. *He had his pianist at last . . .*

CHAPTER TWO

'Nom?'

'C'est égal,' the pianist answered, and shrugged with difficulty because his hands were handcuffed behind him. *'Flic . . . Gestapo, hein?'*

Peipe sucked his teeth. The prisoner's French was heavily accented. He played a hunch. 'Neither,' he answered in German. 'I'm from the *Abwehr*.'

The burly, hard-faced prisoner gave a faint sigh of relief at the information that his interrogator was not from the dreaded Gestapo.

'You might as well undo these,' he said in a pure Berlin working-class accent, indicating the handcuffs. 'It's not as if I'm going to jump you with those two ugly gorillas of yours breathing down my neck, is it?' He nodded at the two burly *Feldgendarmen* standing at either side of the door, the silver crescents of their calling gleaming around their necks.

'All right,' Peipe said. 'But no funny business, mind you.' He beckoned the nearest gendarme across. 'Undo the cuffs,' he commanded.

The man hesitated. 'It's against regulations, sir, during the interrogation of a prisoner who has been found with arms in his possession, sir,' he said sourly.

'Thank you for your information, Corporal,' Peipe answered. 'But please let me make the decisions here, will you?'

The policeman flushed hotly, and without another word unlocked the cuffs.

The prisoner grinned up at him. 'That was a nice kick up the arse for you, bull, wasn't it?' he said cockily, and rubbed his red, gnarled wrists to restore the circulation.

'All right,' Peipe cut into the exchange. 'Let's get on with it. What's your name?'

'I'll tell you that, Captain, but that's all I'll tell you. I'll warn you here and now I'm not the kind who makes bargains. Don't expect any betrayals or deals from me.'

'We'll see about that in due course,' Peipe said, trying to

make his voice threatening and ominous. He knew the type well. The prisoner was one of those tough working-class men who had formed the backbone of the illegal SPD and KPD* underground in Germany; he would be an exceedingly hard nut to crack.

'My name is Maydag, Franz. I was born in Berlin in 1902.'

'Then you are a German, after all,' Peipe said excitedly, sensing again that he had really landed a big fish this time; he was onto something really interesting. A German working illegally in Belgium. The prisoner was obviously not just another resistance worker.

Maydag smiled cheekily. 'You didn't think I was one of those nasty filthy Belgies, did you, Captain, eh? They won't even go down to the latrine to take a piss.'

'Yes, yes, I know that, Maydag. Let's get on with it. You realise that you are in a very serious position. Not only have you been caught red-handed operating an illegal radio transmitter, but you have also been found in possession of highly confidential military information.'

'My ration card is fake too,' Maydag said as cocky as ever. 'I bought it from a chap outside the *Gare du Nord* for two hundred francs. Cheap, I think—'

'Maydag,' Peipe cut in harshly. 'They could stand you against the wall at St Gilles Prison tomorrow morning at dawn and shoot you as a spy on the evidence I've already got against you. Don't you realise that you might have a chance, if you tell us where you get your information and who you are working for?'

Maydag poked a thumb like a sausage against his broad chest. 'Captain, do what you like, threaten me till you're blue in the face, but I'm not going to sing. This particular bird hasn't got a song for you.' He sat back in his chair, as if the whole matter was settled.

Peipe studied the prisoner for what seemed a long time. There was no sound in the tight little room save for the steady breathing of the prisoner and the muffled clatter of the shunting trains from outside. The man's face was scarred and battered as if he had taken his share of blows in his time; he had been through the mill, that was obvious. Yet Peipe knew that in the end, however tough they were, they always sang once the Gestapo began to work on them.

*The German Socialist and Communist Parties, both banned under Hitler.

He broke the heavy silence so abruptly that one of the policemen guarding the door started. 'Maydag, I'm not going to play around with you any longer. I need your information and I'm going to get it, do you understand?'

Maydag shrugged carelessly.

'But don't think I'm going to dirty my hands upon you personally.'

'Yes, you fine gents of the *Abwehr* wouldn't do anything like that, would you?' the prisoner sneered, his dark eyes blazing suddenly, though Peipe had caught a hint of sudden fear. 'You'll let the other lot – these rotten sadistic bastards – do your dirty work for you, eh?'

Peipe squeezed the flesh at the bridge of his rather long sharp nose, as if abruptly he were very tired. 'I don't approve of their methods, Maydag. Never have done and never will do. But you can't make an omelette without breaking eggs–and you know too much for me to be put off by moral scruples. They'll get what I want to know out of you sooner or later, never fear.'

'So it's going to be the Gestapo after all, eh?'

Peipe nodded glumly. One of the main reasons he had left the Berlin Justice Department was that he could not stand working any longer with 'Gestapo' Mueller, the head of the Secret Police. The man had thought the only means of obtaining information from a prisoner was by beating or torturing him. But now he could not afford to be squeamish: Germany was at war, and fighting for her very existence. His personal feelings were unimportant.

Again a heavy silence fell upon the little upstairs room, while both men weighed each other up.

Finally Peipe said, 'I'll make a deal with you, Maydag. Tell me what I want to know and I'll see you're sent to St Gilles as an ordinary member of the Resistance. From there they'll send you to Germany, and with a bit of luck you could survive the war.'

'In Dachau, perhaps?' Maydag sneered. But his old fire was missing. It was as if he were seriously considering Peipe's offer. Whether from fear of Gestapo torturers or because he'd been offered a chance of survival, Peipe didn't know.

'I urge you to accept my offer, Maydag,' Peipe persisted, sensing that the pianist was beginning to weaken. 'Once we leave this room, the matter will be out of my hands. I'll have to report to higher headquarters and they won't hesitate to use the – er – most stringent measures to make you talk.'

'I know, I know,' the prisoner said, suddenly hanging his head as if abruptly he were fully aware of what Peipe was saying. 'Electric shock to your nuts, broom handles stuck up your arse, pissing in your mouth. I know it all well, Captain!'

Involuntarily Peipe bit his bottom lip. The pianist had been through it all before; obviously he knew all the Gestapo's dirty tricks. Suddenly he was disgusted at what he was being forced to do; he wished he could be back in the cleaner air of the front.

He pulled himself together urgently. 'Well, Maydag,' he snapped, his voice toneless, 'are you ready to talk?'

Glumly the prisoner nodded, his head still bent, as if he were ashamed to show his face to his interrogator.

'Good. Who are you working for?'

Maydag did not seem to hear his question, and Peipe was forced to repeat it.

Slowly Maydag staggered to his feet, his face hidden from Peipe's gaze. 'If you'll draw back that blackout curtain for a minute, *Herr Hauptmann*, I'll show you,' he mumbled.

'Show me?'

'Yes.'

Peipe nodded to one of the *Gendarmen*. 'Do as he says,' he commanded.

'But the blackout regs, sir?' the man protested.

'Stick them up your arse!' Peipe snapped hotly, angry at the cop, himself, the prisoner, the whole rotten world. 'Do as I say, man – and quick!'

The policeman leant his rifle against the wall, and striding across to the window, drew back the curtain to reveal the blacked-out silhouette of the Belgian capital.

'Now get on with it, Maydag,' Peipe said, rising to his feet, wondering curiously what the prisoner thought he could show him.

'Well, it's like this—' The prisoner never ended his sentence. With one last desperate burst of energy, the pianist dived forward. Before Peipe or the two policemen could stop him, he crashed head-first through the window, scattering broken glass and trailing behind him a wild shriek of despair. Peipe, paralysed with shock, stood there helplessly. The thud as the prisoner's body hit the hard cobbles three storeys below snapped him from his reveries. He rushed to the window.

In a blaze of yellow light from the window he could see the prisoner's body stretched out below, both arms flung out melodramatically. Even before the excited shouts from beneath told him that the prisoner was dead, he knew there could be no hope that Maydag could have survived that fall. The pianist had taken his secret with him. Now it would be up to Berlin to look into the matter.

Behind him at the window the policeman who had removed Maydag's handcuffs said, his voice full of barely concealed, malicious joy, 'I told you, sir, it was against regs to remove the cuffs. Now you can see what the result is.'

Peipe ignored him. Angrily he picked up the old-fashioned, long-stemmed phone on the desk and rapped in French to the operator: 'M'selle, I want you to get me this number in Berlin at once. Top priority. Yes, you heard me correctly . . . top priority . . .'

CHAPTER THREE

'*Impossible!* I don't believe it. I just don't believe it,' the Field-Marshal exclaimed, shocked, the cheeks of his long wooden face flushed. 'My God, it means we have a traitor right at the top here, somewhere in Berlin – at the very top!'

Captain Peipe remained silent. There was nothing he could say to the outraged Chief of the High Command. One hour before, unshaven, hungry and exhausted, he had arrived at Tempelhof Airport and had been driven straight away to the *Abwehr* H.Q. in Berlin's Tirpitzstrasse. At the main entrance an officer of the guard had tried to make him open his briefcase which contained the precious documents he had seized in the Rue d'Atrebas. Peipe had refused, and when the officer had declared angrily that he, Peipe, could not enter the *Abwehr* H.Q. without his briefcase being checked, Peipe had drawn his pistol and snapped: 'You try to open this briefcase, Lieutenant, and I will shoot you.'

The Lieutenant had given in, and said he would conduct Peipe to the officer in charge of the Belgian Desk. Peipe had said he didn't want to see some subordinate officer; he wanted to see either Admiral Canaris himself or his deputy, Colonel Bentivegni.

Canaris had not been in at that early hour. But Bentivegni, the Austrian spy-hunter, had at once recognised the vital importance of the seized documents. He had taken Peipe over to the High Command building almost immediately. Within minutes, Keitel, his tunic undone and his face still unshaven, was listening thunderstruck to Peipe's story of the night's happenings in Brussels.

'But where do they get such material,' Keitel exclaimed angrily, slapping the pile of documents with his heavy paw. 'Plans of our new Messerschmidt fighter, detailed statistics of our tank production, a complete exposé of this winter's campaign in Russia. They must have men in every important H.Q. and Ministry in the capital.' He glared around the walls of his big office, as if he half expected to see agents come tumbling out of the dark panelling at any moment. With an effort he pulled himself together. 'But who are they working for, eh?' he demanded. 'Who are the paymasters – the Tommies or the Ivans? Tell me that!'

'*Herr Generalfeldmarschall*,' Bentivegni said in that soft, soothing Viennese manner of his, 'you must realise that we have had only a matter of minutes to ponder that question ourselves.'

'And?' Keitel demanded, unappeased by the Austrian's charm.

'Well, it is clear that the group discovered by Captain Peipe was not of the local resistance, though the woman maintained before she' – the Colonel coughed nervously, as if it were not quite done to talk about death – 'succumbed, that she believed she had been working for the *Armée Blanche*. But the other three were all Germans. Therefore we can safely conclude—'

'Oh, get on with it, Colonel,' Keitel interrupted brutally.

'We can conclude, therefore, that they were all connected with some spy organisation or other. Now in the Tirpitzstrasse, there are already two groups of thought about which organisation they belonged to. One maintains that as most of the material seems to relate to the Russian front, they were working for the Reds.'

'And the other school of thought?'

'The British. They have always had a monopoly in the West, virtually since World War One.'

'The Tommies, eh?' Field-Marshal Keitel rubbed his heavy unshaven jaw thoughtfully. Suddenly he stared hard at Peipe. 'And you, Captain, what do you think?'

'I beg your pardon, Field-Marshal?'

'Are you deaf? Or dumb? To which theory do you subscribe: East or West?' Keitel rapped in that unpleasant manner which had made him the most-hated officer in the High Command.

'I don't really know, sir,' Peipe answered, feeling himself flush. 'It has all happened so suddenly.' He pushed on resolutely. 'All I know is that there is one devil of a leak somewhere here in the Reich – probably here in Berlin – and we must plug it as quickly as possible before we are flooded out.'

'Agreed,' Keitel snapped. 'If the Führer ever gets to know of this, heads will roll – and one of them could well be that of that Father Christmas of yours over in Tirpitzstrasse.'

Now it was Colonel Bentivegni's turn to flush hotly, at the contemptuous reference to his own beloved chief, Admiral Canaris, whom the SS called Father Christmas on account of his shock of white hair and soft, 'un-Germanic' manners.

Keitel did not notice. He never noticed such things. Turning to Peipe again, he declared: 'All right, *Herr Hauptmann*, after you have eaten and shaved, you will go across to the Prinzalbrechtstrasse—'

'Number Ten, sir?' Peipe interrupted hastily.

'*Naturlich.* What number did you think? There you will contact an official by the name of Stahl. He is the best man we've got over there. He should . . .'

But Captain Peipe was no longer listening. His mind was too concerned with the address. The damned Gestapo was going to be dragged into the business after all . . .

The office on the second floor of the Gestapo H.Q. was sparsely furnished and bare of decoration, save for the framed citations on the walls, which indicated that the emaciated man bent over the bubbling coffee pot on the stove in the corner had been around a long time.

'Yes,' *Obersturmbannführer* Stahl croaked in his hoarse boozer's voice, as if he could read Peipe's mind, 'I was a cop under the Kaiser, under Hindenburg too, and now under Hitler. If Thaelmann* ever comes into power, I'll be a cop under him as well. I'm a professional, you see, my dear Captain.'

He turned round and beamed at Peipe, showing his long yellow teeth, set in a wrinkled leathery face. He put the steaming cup of coffee on the bare desk and poured a hefty slug of cognac into it. 'You too, Captain?'

* Leader of the pre-war German Communist Party.

Peipe shook his head. 'It's only nine o'clock, *Obersturmbannführer.*'

Stahl took a sip of the fiery mixture, and said in that hoarse croak of his: 'It's never too early or too late for me, Captain. Coffee and cognac are my medicine – they're the only things which keep me from kicking off.'

He saw the puzzled look on Peipe's face, and gestured at his throat. 'The bone-patchers tell me I've got cancer of the throat. Coffee and cognac are the medicine they prescribed. Whether it does any good or not, I don't know, but the cognac certainly keeps me happy.' With that he took another sip of the mixture.

Peipe told himself that this was the strangest Gestapo man he had ever met. There was none of the flashy brutality of the usual member of the Secret Police. He felt he could work with this man.

Stahl finished his coffee-cognac with a flourish and sighed appreciatively. 'Now then, Captain, where's the fire?' he asked, sitting back in his chair.

In a few hurried sentences, Peipe told him what had happened the previous night and what Keitel's reaction had been. Stahl listened in silence, breaking it only to ask what the *Abwehr* jargon-word 'pianist' meant.

For what seemed a long time after Peipe had finished, the Gestapo official sat deep in thought in his chair, his skinny face without any trace of emotion. Outside in the corridor there was the stamp of boots, harsh, quick and self-important, full of brutal pride.

Finally Stahl spoke. 'We must be patient, Captain. As you rightly assume, they must have a spy, or spies, here in Berlin in one of the ministries or H.Q.s. Good, but for the moment he can do nothing. Why?' Stahl answered his own question. 'Because he lacks a . . . pianist, as you call it, and a music box. Without a pianist he cannot pass on his information to his bosses, whoever they might be. So we must wait until the pianist is found and begins playing his music box once more. In the meantime I shall set my smart-arsed young intellectuals working on the messages you found in Brussels. Perhaps the nature of the messages might help them to pinpoint the particular H.Q. or Ministry from which our spy is working.'

'Good idea,' Peipe agreed hastily. 'If there is nothing, say, on naval or foreign affairs, we can cut out the Navy H.Q. and the Foreign Office.'

'Exactly. Now, once we have established that particular

point, and once a new pianist begins working, we are in a much better position to find out how the messages are passed from Berlin to Brussels.'

'Well, they are certainly not passed from here to there by radio. The Air Force listening station at Kranz reports there is no illegal radio traffic coming from Berlin.'

'Good,' Stahl croaked. 'So that means the information is passed by letter or courier, and that narrows down the field a bit more. There can't be that many people writing or travelling to Brussels from one particular ministry or H.Q., can there?'

Peipe nodded his agreement. 'So the plan is that I go back to Brussels and wait for a new pianist to start playing, while you conduct the search operation here in Berlin?'

'Yes.' With a hoarse groan, Stahl, levered his long, wasted body from the chair and went over to the bubbling coffee pot on the stove. Again he poured himself a cup of the steaming black mixture and added a generous slug of his 'medicine'. 'That is about all we can do for the time being. Wait and drink English tea, as they used to say when I was a boy. But believe you me, my dear Captain, when we have our spy and the new pianist, we won't be finished by a long chalk.' He tapped his long beaky nose. 'My old honker here tells me there is a much bigger fish behind all this. Much bigger . . .'

Jean-Pierre couldn't help thinking that the new recruit looked more like an Englishman than a Belgian, with his tall athletic frame, bright blue eyes and long ash-blond hair. But he told himself that probably the Belgian had Flemish blood in his veins like so many of the French-speaking Walloons from over the border.

Now it had begun to rain. The sand of the beach began to run to thick goo beneath their boots, and the water sluicing from the white chalk cliffs formed channels and tributaries that coursed disconsolately downwards. Ahead of them a pair of wild ducks fled, honking hoarsely, their wings flapping in the pouring rain.

Jean-Pierre seized the Belgian's arm and guided him to the shelter of one of the beach-huts. The rain drummed furiously on its tin roof and Jean-Pierre had to shout his question above the racket: 'How long have you been in France, Belgian?'

The other man wiped the rain-drops from his face and

shouted back, 'Well, I haven't got the pox yet from one of your whores, so it can't be so long, *Frenchman*.'

Jean-Pierre laughed in spite of the miserable weather. The Belgian had a sense of humour – for a Belgian. 'All right, comrade. But you see, even we French Communists are chauvinists at heart.'

The young Belgian laughed easily, showing excellent teeth, as if he hadn't a care in the world on this wet, cold September day. 'But, comrade, you didn't ask me to come all this way to this God-forsaken dump – give me Ostend any time – to pass the time of day, did you?'

Jean-Pierre nodded hastily. 'Of course not, comrade. I hear you are a technician?' He looked at the other man's handsome open face.

'Yes. Up to the spring I worked for the cheeseheads at Philips, Eindhoven, in their radio development plant. But when the Boche started to round up the cheeseheads for work in Germany, I decided it was time that I went underground. I've been illegal ever since. The Party in Antwerp supplied me with money and rations.'

Jean-Pierre shouted against the drumming of the rain, 'Yes, I know. The comrades in Antwerp told me. That's why I asked them to send you across the border. You are a Party member, a Belgian, and have the technical know-how we need.'

'For what?' the Belgian asked without any great curiosity.

Jean-Pierre told himself the man was like all those who had been illegal for a long time; they were no longer particularly curious about the mysteries with which they were confronted daily in their underground existence. 'The Party needs somebody who can learn to play a music box pretty quickly – a pianist, in other words.'

'A what?'

Jean-Pierre waited until another pair of wild ducks beat low across the heaving dark-green sea, heading for the rushes, before he answered: 'We need a radio operator . . .'

TWO: THE ORCHESTRA IS RED

CHAPTER ONE

She had not yet come.

He paused and looked down at her spread across the big double bed. Jeanette was a big woman – he always thought of her as a slimmer version of a Rubens model. To himself he called her 'the Flemish Mare'. Her breasts were very large and protuberant, but she had excellent legs, long and slim, though, like the rest of her body, their skin was rough, as if she didn't bathe enough.

'*Chéri*,' she whispered, her eyes screwed tightly closed under the damp blonde hair which stuck to her forehead.

Peipe whispered another of those absurd French endearments in her ear – 'my little attic mouse, my sweet rabbit' – which made him wince when he recollected them later. He squeezed both her nipples routinely and commenced thrusting once more, though his heart was not in it.

Lena had been different – sophisticated, elegant, independent. But Lena was long dead, and the Boy, too, killed in the first air-raid of the war in the supposedly safe Freiburg to which he, fool that he was, had evacuated them from the dangers of the capital. Now there was no Lena; only a succession of Jeanettes.

He thrust harder. She was beginning to moan and thresh about the bed now. It took all his strength to hold her. She was a strong girl. Her legs closed around the small of his back like a vice. 'Little sweet hen,' he cried squeezing her breasts.

Suddenly she came, with a tremendous, body-racking shudder. Her heart began to thump furiously. It always did, and it frightened him; he feared she might have a heart attack. She relaxed her vice-like grip and flopped on the bed, her breasts heaving as if she had just run a very long race.

'Thank God,' he whispered to himself, and rose from the bed. He looked out of the window at the spiked outline of morning Brussels. It had begun to snow. Winter had begun.

'Don't leave me, Horst,' she whispered, her eyes still tightly closed.

'Duty calls,' he answered, and looked back at her. Her mouth hung open like an idiot's. He looked away. Jeanette revolted him in a way, with her peasant innocence, just as he was revolted by his own guile. Still, he must have someone and she was as good as the next one. 'I must telephone the office, my kitten,' he said over his shoulder as he walked into the next room.

Fat Heinz, his sergeant, answered the phone himself.

'Well, you fat rogue,' Peipe demanded with false joviality, 'how was the night?'

'Cold, sir,' Fat Heinz, who weighed all of one hundred kilos, answered with a barely suppressed yawn.

'You've got plenty of bacon and lard on you, Heinz,' Peipe commented, and looked out of the window. It was snowing hard now. The flakes were striking the glass like white tracer.

'Not a whisper, sir,' Fat Heinz gave him the information he sought. 'The boys here say nothing and Kranz reports the same. The air's clear. We might as well close up shop for all the action we're getting.'

Peipe caught a glimpse of Jeanette in the mirror. She was staring at his back with that cowlike look on her pale, pretty face. With his heel he slammed the door shut. She didn't speak a word of German, but all the same he had to be careful.

'Thanks, Heinz. Well, you can go to bed now. I'll see you at five this evening.'

'Alone, sir?'

'Alone what?'

'To go to bed.'

'That's your problem, you fat rogue. It's going to be a long boring winter, you might as well find some little Belgian bed-hare to keep your beer-belly warm for you.'

Heinz chuckled and hung up.

Slowly Peipe began to dress for another day of war. Finally he was fully clothed save for his tunic, which was in the bedroom. Jeanette was already gone, as was her wont, without a good-bye, but with the rations he always gave her carefully tucked away in her carrier bag. He was glad. He sat on the stained rumpled bed and began to eat a bar of chocolate for breakfast – somehow she had overlooked it. With an empty numb feeling he stared out at the driving snow. He'd have to survive another winter. 'But for what?' he asked his own reflection in the fly-specked mirror of the wardrobe. His reflection made no reply.

The Grand Chef stepped out of a doorway twenty metres before she reached the little bistro where they had arranged to meet the previous day. Slipping his arm under hers as if he had known her for years, he began to walk rapidly in the opposite direction. 'We'll go over to the bar near the Palace of Justice,' he said, in his strangely accented French.

She looked at him. The Grand Chef, the only name she knew him by, was about thirty-five, and not exactly handsome, with his heavy powerful features and wavy, cropped blond hair; yet he had appeal and charm for women. With him she always felt safe. He had an inner strength that allayed fears and made everything seem simple. If she had still been going to church, he would have been the kind of father-confessor she'd have liked.

He seemed to read her mind, as always. 'Never meet regularly in any one place, Jeanette,' he explained, his face buried deep in the collar of his heavy black coat, against the driving snow. 'It's one of the basic rules of conspiracy.'

'I see,' she said, telling herself that the Grand Chef knew everything.

They walked in silence until they reached the bar. He pushed back the big felt curtain and entered first in the German fashion. The place was crowded and heavy with the sweet-smelling blue smoke of *Boule Nationale* cigarettes.

'Rule two,' he whispered in her ear as he led her to an empty table. 'Always meet in a crowd. Treffs in empty places are dangerous.'

As polite as ever, he pulled back a chair for her to sit down. She noticed he positioned himself with his back to the door, as if he had no fear of being arrested. All the same, he could watch anyone who came in, in the big mirror behind the zinc-covered bar.

The waiter came over, and he ordered a coffee for her without asking her if she wanted one, and a Pernod for himself. It was a *jour avec**; the bar could serve alcohol.

He let her take a drink of her coffee, and then he asked without further delay, 'Well, what did you find out?'

She shrugged. 'Not much. There doesn't seem to be much going on, as far as I could see. He left the office two hours earlier last night, so you can assume that he didn't have much to do, and he didn't seem to be in a particular hurry this morning.'

'Did he make his usual call this morning?' the Grand Chef

* During the war no alcohol was served in Belgium in bars and cafes on alternative days.

asked, his eyes still on the mirror behind the bar.

She nodded a little hesitantly.

'What did he say?'

'I don't like listening to him like that,' she said.

The Grand Chef looked at her; for a moment there was a flash of fire in his dark intelligent eyes, then it was gone as quickly as it had appeared. He said nothing.

'Oh, well, he chatted a bit with that fat sergeant of his,' she went on after a moment. 'Usual men's talk. Then he asked, how was the night?'

'What?'

She told him again.

'Repeat his words exactly in German,' he said.

'*Wie war die Nacht?*' she said reluctantly. The Grand Chef himself had ordered her never to let it be known that she could speak German fluently.

'In that tone – bored, careless?' he persisted.

'Yes, there was nothing excited about it – simply routine.' She sipped the ersatz coffee and wrinkled her nose at the taste. What she wouldn't give for a cup of good old pre-war *cafe-filtre*!

'I'll bring you a pound of real coffee beans next time I meet you,' the Grand Chef said.

'You notice everything, don't you?'

He laughed easily. 'Most things, I suppose. For instance you like him – the Boche, I mean – a lot, don't you?'

She nodded slowly, as if she were thinking hard about his words. 'He is not a bad man,' she said at last.

'He's a Boche.'

'But he's unlike the rest,' she said hastily. 'He's been badly hurt. His wife and son – then his arm. 'She shrugged her plump, well-covered shoulders a little helplessly. 'I'm afraid, I think . . . I love him.'

The Grand Chef did not respond. Instead he said, 'All right, finish your coffee and move out. I'll follow in five minutes.'

As she walked out into the driving snow, her shoulders bent almost sadly, Trepper told himself that sooner or later she'd have to be killed.

'I am going to give you a lecture, comrade,' the heavy-set man with the wavy cropped hair and strange French accent said slowly.

The tall, athletic Belgian nodded, but said nothing. They kept on walking through the snow-bound park with its stark-black skeletal trees.

'Once the pianist begins to work his music box,' the heavy-set man commenced his lecture, 'he is as vulnerable as an infantryman going over the top and facing the first bursts of enemy machine-gun fire. I do not wish to scare you right from the start, but to sit at the music box and keep playing it, when you know that all around you the enemy is alerted and working frantically to locate you, takes a special kind of courage. I hope you have got it, comrade?'

'I think I have,' the Belgian said, his voice and his face revealing neither fear nor pride.

'You must be on your guard constantly. Loiterers, post-office workers repairing a broken cable, men carrying heavy suitcases – and naturally the detector vans. In short everything and anything could lead to your arrest, if you're not on your toes all the time. I know, comrade, believe me. I've been illegal for over twenty years.'

'I shall take care.' The Belgian paused in mid-stride and touched his face gently. 'It's too pretty a turnip to have it chopped off by the gent in the tailcoat and silk hat just yet.'

The heavy-set man laughed softly at the Belgian's reference to the traditional dress of the German public executioner. 'Good. Then you are warned, comrade. Now to details. You will play the music box according to this pattern.' He took out a scrap of paper and gave it to the Belgian. 'There you have a series of six wavelengths and thirty call signals. You will use wavelength A to send the Centre your first message, then switch to wavelength B, and so on. If you have more than six messages, you move back to wavelength A for your seventh message and follow the same routine as before. Understood?'

'Understood.'

'Fine.' The heavy-set man gave the Belgian the benefit of his magnetic smile, which seemed to express the man's undoubted strength and vitality, although it was obvious to the Belgian that he was living under a lot of pressure. 'Now you will follow a similar pattern with the call signals, using a different one for each new day.'

'Some months have thirty-one days,' the younger man objected.

'I know. On that day the pianist will be free. We'll find a

girl for you – a trustworthy loyal female comrade – to take care of your needs.' He winked at the Belgian.

'Only once a month?' The Belgian gave a mock sigh. 'I'll never be able to stand it!'

'Wait till you've had a week of nights at the music box,' the heavy-set man said. 'You'll be only too glad to hit the sack and get some sleep.'

'I doubt that,' the Belgian said sourly.

The other man ignored the comment. His face was serious again. 'Now remember this, comrade. Your main aim is to keep the Boche *Funkabwehr* off your neck. When you start playing tomorrow night, they'll be on to you straight off. From then onwards, they'll be after you every night, and thanks to their damned curfew we can't give you any look-outs to watch out for the bastards. In essence you'll be on your own. So keep on your toes. And one last tip: never play the music box too long on any one wavelength – it will give the Boche bastards more of a chance to locate you. Understood?'

'Understood.'

'Fine. then, that's that. You won't see me again, I should imagine. But the girl'll keep me in touch with you.'

'What girl?'

'The one you're going to fuck on the thirty-first day.' The heavy-set man held out his hand. 'Good luck.'

A moment later he was walking swiftly through the snow, back the way they had come, leaving the Belgian staring at his broad powerful back and wondering . . .

CHAPTER TWO

Captain Peipe's prediction to Fat Heinz that it would be a long, boring winter proved to be false. On the Saturday before the Christmas of 1941, he was celebrating his thirty-fifth birthday with Jeanette and was well into his third bottle of champagne when the phone rang suddenly in his living room.

Jeanette, who was tipsy, and had already removed her dress and was now trying to look sexy and provocative in the black silk underwear and stockings he had bought her in Paris, pouted her scarlet lips. 'Don't answer it, Horst,' she said thickly. 'I bet it's one of those crazy pigs who phone and try to annoy German officers in the middle of the night. And they call that *resistance.*'

Captain Peipe was inclined to agree with her, but when the phone continued to ring and ring, he gave in and picked it up. 'Peipe,' he rapped, a little annoyed. If Jeanette overcame her tipsiness, it would take him half the night to make her come.

'*Herr Hauptmann,* thank God I reached you,' Heinz cried excitedly at the other end. 'I thought you might have taken a sleeping pill again.'

'Where's the fire?' Peipe cut in harshly.

'But it's important, vitally important, sir,' Heinz protested.

'What?'

'There's a new p-pianist on the air, sir,' Heinz stuttered. 'Kranz just phoned through. They picked him up about thirty minutes ago.'

'Oh, my sweet arse!' Peipe groaned, and put down his champagne glass suddenly, unaware that behind his back Jeanette had thrown off her drunkenness and was listening to the conversation intently.

'Yes, a new one, in our area somewhere, and a completely new handwriting.'

'*Handwriting?*' Peipe queried, puzzled by the word.

'Yes, that's what the experts call the pianist's style of transmission. Kranz says he's going to be a tough nut to crack, *Herr Hauptmann.*' Heinz groaned miserably. 'The bastard will have us out tramping the streets again in this weather. It's going to be a shitty happy Christmas, sir, don't you agree?'

And Captain Peipe could do nothing else but agree with his subordinate's mournful comment.

Two days later, Stahl called from Berlin. Even his increasing hoarseness could not quite conceal the note of triumph in his voice. 'We've got 'em!' he announced without any preliminaries.

'Who?' Peipe asked.

'The traitors here in Berlin. My tame intellectuals have worked out where the leaks are.'

'Excellent. Where?'

'Fat Hermann* is going to burst a gut when he hears,' Stahl said with a throaty chuckle.

* Reich-Marshal Hermann Goering, known as 'Fat Hermann' on account of his enormous girth, head of the German *Luftwaffe* in World War II.

'You mean the Reich Air Ministry?'

'Right.' At the other end, Peipe could hear the cognac bottle, which always stood on Stahl's desk, being uncorked, and there was the sound of liquid being poured into a glass. 'Just took a little extra medicine to celebrate,' Stahl explained a moment later. 'There's more to come, Peipe, old friend. Not only have we pin-pointed the Ministry, but we think we know who the traitors are.'

'Tell me more,' Peipe said eagerly.

'It's a beautiful set-up,' Stahl said, equally excited, 'and there's going to be one sweet hell of a scandal if it ever gets out. You see, there's a whole bunch of them – elegant high-born ladies, and gentlemen officers – centred round a major in the Air Ministry.'

'What's his name?'

'Absolute top secret, Peipe,' Stahl answered. 'But you're in this as deep as I am, so I think I can tell you. He's called Schulze-Boysen, and not only is he a personal protégé of Fat Hermann, he's no less than old Fork-beard's nephew.'

'Fork-beard?' Peipe asked puzzled.

'Of course, I forget that you've still got egg-shell behind your ears, Peipe. He was before your time. Fork-beard was Admiral Tirpitz.'

Peipe whistled softly. 'The founder of the Imperial Navy?' he said.

'No less,' Stahl said gleefully. 'Now you can see what I mean about one sweet hell of a scandal.'

'You can say that again, Stahl. But what's your plan from here on?'

'All I need now is some evidence linking them with that new pianist that has turned up in your area, and I'll be onto them like a shot. I've already spoken to the *Reichsheini** about it and he'll approve the arrests, once we have that link. You'll be hearing from me, Peipe. *Prost!*' There was the sound of more cognac being poured into a glass.

'*Prost!*'

The line went dead.

On Christmas Day, Peipe was lounging on the sofa listening to the carols from the Homeland on the radio when his bell rang. He had just eaten the heavy traditional Christmas dinner, and had made love to Jeanette, who was fast asleep and snor-

* Heinrich Himmler, head of the SS and the German Police.

ing in the bedroom. He had been looking forward to this moment when he could think of Lena and the Boy and other Christmases. As a result he was annoyed by the disturbance. Muttering angrily to himself, he went to the door and flung it open. He gasped with surprise. Dressed in his best black SS uniform, complete with his First World War medals, his skinny shoulders lightly powdered with snow, Stahl stood there, grinning at him.

'You!' Peipe exclaimed.

'Who do you think – Santa Claus? Now then, where's that good French cognac of yours, Peipe? My throat feels like the bottom of a parrot's cage.' Roughly he elbowed the surprised Captain to one side and headed straight for the cognac bottle on the table. Without asking, he filled himself a glass right to the brim and drained it in one mighty greedy gulp.

'Be my guest,' Peipe said, half annoyed, half amused.

'Think I will,' the Gestapo man said jovially. 'This is what I really call a cognac – not like that gnat's piss that masquerades as cognac in Berlin.' He filled his glass again and sat down. 'You chaps do yourself well in foreign parts, Peipe,' he observed. 'The Thousand-Year Reich looks a little shabby in comparison with this decadent occupied country.'

Peipe sat down facing him. Stahl was obviously very pleased with himself; normally he suppressed his true feelings about the National Socialist State. 'Well, Stahl, I don't suppose you came all this way to drink my firewater and make highly treasonable remarks to an officer of counter-intelligence who is duty-bound to report them to the appropriate authority?'

Stahl grinned. 'No, Captain, I didn't, though if you've got a couple of bottles of that good stuff handy, you might let me have them for the trip back!'

'Trip back?'

'Yes, I've come to carry you off from this decadent hell,' he nodded happily at Jeanette's shoes which were thrown carelessly under the chair where she had eaten. 'They even gave me the *Reichsheini's* personal Junkers to fly you back.'

'To where?' Peipe said, bewildered, his anger mounting at the way Stahl was playing with him.

Stahl took a sip of his cognac. 'To Berlin.'

'But why, man? Don't talk in riddles.'

Stahl put down his glass and beamed at the red-faced Captain, obviously unable to conceal his triumph any longer. 'We've got them, Peipe,' he announced in a hasty eager croak.'

The whole bunch of them. Yesterday morning, the customs guards at Aachen nabbed their courier on the Berlin–Brussels express. He was carrying documents stolen from the Air Ministry. Pity we couldn't have followed him right through to his contact man here, but we'll get the info out of him, no doubt. In the end they all sing when my boys start working on them. It's a fact of life.' He drained his cognac. 'All right, Captain, don't look at me like that. I didn't make the system . . . Now come on, get dressed and pack a case.' He grinned evilly, showing his long yellow teeth. 'And if you want to say good-bye to your lady-love in the appropriate fashion, I'll put cotton-wool in my ears and concentrate on your cognac.'

But Captain Horst Peipe had never felt less like making love. With Jeanette sobbing at his side, he packed his bag mechanically and unseeingly, his mind full of the horror which lay ahead of him in Number 10, Prinzalbrechtstrasse.

'It's a very bad business, very bad indeed,' the Grand Chef said, staring miserably across the white waste of the Grand Square.

Jeanette, equally miserable, said nothing. Her mind was full of Horst.

'Of course, we have taken immediate measures,' he continued, as if talking to himself. 'We alarmed the courier's contact-man immediately. He's gone underground. Anyone else who had dealings with the Berlin network has done the same. Even if those swine of the Gestapo get them to talk, they can only incriminate themselves, not us. Besides, I'm taking measures to move our whole organisation here to somewhere else. I'll notify you in due course.'

The Grand Chef turned, his miserable look gone, and pressed her cold ungloved hand reassuringly. 'Don't worry, everything will turn out all right.' He looked down at her reddened fingers. 'I must see if I can't get you a pair of good gloves on the black market as soon as possible. This cold will spoil your hands.'

'Thank you,' she whispered miserably.

'Now then, to you, my dear,' the Grand Chef said in his normal confident, reassuring tone. 'You don't look well, not well at all, you know.'

'I know,' she confessed. 'I feel blue.'

'I know a remedy for that, Jeanette,' he said swiftly.

'What?'

'A new affair. "New love, new life," Goethe once said, and he should have known, the old devil – he was at it right up to his death-bed.' He smiled down at her.

She looked at him, her pretty face puzzled. 'I don't . . . understand,' she stuttered.'

'Your Boche has gone to Berlin, probably to help torture those poor bastards the Gestapo have taken—'

'Horst would never do anything like that,' she protested.

'It is his duty, and a German soldier always does his duty, you know that,' he replied firmly. Then raising his hand to stop her protesting any further, he said: 'I've got a man for you. My new pianist. He's a handsome brute and should have no trouble finding himself a girl. But I can't have him running the risk of going into bars and nightclubs looking for one. You know the dangers you can run in such places. Besides, he's only going to have one night off a month. So how can we keep a young fellow like that happy, eh, Jeanette?' He paused, and then answered his own question in that overwhelming, supremely confident manner of his. 'I'll tell you. By giving him what he needs in bed, safely, and on the premises.'

'But I couldn't do that,' she protested, her face paler than ever.

'You did it before with the Boche, and the ones who came before him. You have always done what the Party has wanted you to do, Jeanette. 'And,' he added with a twinkle in his dark eye, 'I don't think you have altogether disliked it, eh?'

'But with the others before, it was different. Now . . . now,' she sought desperately for the right words, 'it would be like betraying him, betraying Horst.'

'There are no buts, Jeanette,' he snapped, iron in his voice suddenly. 'You will obey Party instructions. You will attend to the young man's needs in bed and you will act as my contact with him. And that's that. Now off you go. We've been standing here together for too long as it is . . .'

He had not gone more than a dozen metres when he stopped and shouted over his shoulder: 'Oh, and I'll remember to get those gloves. You must really take more care of your hands.'

CHAPTER THREE

Fortner hit the man in the blue suit across the face, once, twice, three times, slapping his cheeks back and forth. Then he took off the leather glove with which he protected his well-tended hand on such occasions, and let Bass take over. Bass waited until the prisoner had wiped the blood from his split lips; then he grabbed him by his long blond hair and in one amazingly swift movement (for such a gross person), he pulled his head down and rammed his fat knee right into the prisoner's face.

In the observation room Peipe was watching the first interrogation of the day. He winced. There was no sound coming through from next door, but watching the prisoner's bloody contorted face through the one-way window, Peipe could imagine the agony he was going through.

Bass let the prisoner stagger to his feet again, blood pouring through the fingers clasped over his face. But only for a moment. Again Bass moved with tremendous speed. His knee shot into the prisoner's crotch. The man fell to the tiled floor, writhing back and forth with the pain, his knees drawn up under his chin as if he were in the womb. Bass did not seem even to notice. He walked slowly to the table, the room's sole furniture and sat down on it next to the elegant Fortner. With a hand that looked like a small ham, he picked up the open bottle of beer on the table and took a deep appreciative pull. On the floor the prisoner continued to writhe in agony.

Stahl turned to a pale Peipe. 'So, my dear Captain, you see our famous spy for the first time. Not a pretty sight is he, Major Harro Schulze-Boysen?'

Peipe licked lips suddenly dry and agreed in a low voice.

'You should have seen him when they brought him in here three weeks ago. The very epitome of Aryan beauty – all broad shoulders, blond hair and piercing blue eyes. Just the type the Führer wants for his SS.' Stahl took a sip at his coffee-cognac 'medicine'. 'Not much of the Nordic specimen about him now, I'm afraid.'

Again Peipe agreed in a low voice, his face pale and miserable. It had been a terrible three weeks. Every day in the cellars, watching Stahl's 'experts' working over the suspects:

Ministerial Councillor Harnack, dry and ugly; his wife Mildred, American and equally ugly; Libertas Schulze-Boysen, the Major's wife, pretty, sexy and deathly scared. He had watched them reduced to panic-stricken animals, had seen the fear crawl into them like some small bewildered rodent, and take total possession.

They had all sung, as Stahl had predicted they would. They had told everything, from Libertas's lesbian seduction of important women in order to make them spy for her husband, to Harnack's confession that he had always been a Communist and that he had joined the spy ring because 'I have the conviction that the ideals of the Soviet Union are paving the way for the world's salvation. My aim was the destruction of the Hitler regime by every means available.'

It had been an important admission. As Stahl had commented happily that particular day, 'Well, that takes us a good step further, Peipe, doesn't it? Now at least we know they are working for the Ivans.'

But in all the three, long, weeks of unspeakable torture, the elegant Fortner, and his running-mate, the gross, pig-necked Bass, had still not been able to get the one piece of vital information out of Schulze-Boysen – who was his under-cover boss. According to his statements, which were always full of attacks on the National Socialist system, he had started the ring himself because of his hatred of the Nazis; his only contact with the unknown Russian 'resident' in Occupied Europe was through a series of cut-outs and couriers. As he snarled at Bass during one prolonged interrogation: 'All you can do is to beat the sense out of me until I don't know whether I'm coming or going. But you can't make me tell you the resident's name because I don't damn well know it!'

Now Stahl was to take over the interrogation of the spy ring-leader himself. He took one last puff at his cheap cigarette, and filling a cup half full of coffee and then adding a generous dash of his 'medicine', he nodded to Peipe.

'All right,' he said, 'we'd better get started.'

Reluctantly Peipe followed him out.

Now Schulze-Boysen had begun to sit up again, but his breath was still coming in sharp, pain-stabbed gasps. He glared at the newcomers, his bruised eyes and bloody face set in a look of defiance. Instinctively Peipe knew as he looked at the spy, that they were wasting their time with the Major; they would not get anything out of him. The man was prepared to fight back all the way, and then in defeat would go gladly and bravely to his death.

Stahl nodded to his 'experts', took a sip from his coffee, and said in his hoarse voice: 'My name is Stahl. I am in charge of your interrogation, Major. Like you, I'm under a sentence of death. I intend to get the information out of you before I die. It is as simple as that. Do you understand?' Stahl spoke without any visible emotion, as if he talked about his own death every day.

'Field-Marshal Goering has commanded me to employ all available means to make you talk – he is very upset with you. Herr Himmler has signed the official permit to allow me to use "reinforced interrogation", which means I can have you flogged. In other words, you are completely in my hands. I can do with you what I like and no one will give a damn. Is that clear?'

A hint of colour appeared in the prisoner's thin cheeks. 'What do you think your gorillas have been doing to me for the last three weeks?' he mumbled, with an attempt at contempt. 'I have not talked to them. Why should I do so to you?'

'The answer is very simple,' Stahl said, in no way put out. 'Because I am Stahl, that is why.' Suddenly he reached forward. Without any warning, he grabbed Schulze-Boysen by his long unkempt blond hair and gave him a stinging blow at the base of his nose which sent him back to the floor, choking and retching, the blood pouring in a thick red stream from his ruptured nostrils.

Watching from the corner, Peipe bit his bottom lip. At bottom, then, Stahl was like the rest; all he knew about making a prisoner talk was to use brute force.

But Peipe was to be proven wrong. The blow was just an old habit, the expected calling-card of a policeman introducing himself to a suspect. Stahl, too, had taken the measure of the prisoner; he knew that torture would not work. He was prepared to use other means.

'What if I tell you that your whole attitude is old-fashioned and quite unnecessary,' he said suddenly. 'What would you say to that, Major?'

He took a sip of his coffee and waited for Schulze-Boysen's reaction.

The prisoner looked at him puzzled.

'The courier has already talked,' Stahl continued. 'Has told us everything we want to know about your Brussels set-up. We are ready to arrest the lot of them within the next twenty-four hours.'

Peipe nodded his approval at Stahl's tactic. The courier had managed to commit suicide by biting the veins of his wrists on the first night of his captivity, but the prisoner did not know that.

Schulze-Boysen gave a pathetic parody of his once confident devil-may-care shrug. 'Then why carry on with me?'

'Because we need more details,' Stahl said, searching the prisoner's face for any sign of weakening.

'I think I must have told those apes of yours a thousand times that I do not know anything about any organisation in Belgium. I formed my own organisation. I got into contact with Moscow independently, and was directed to send any information I had via courier to Belgium. That's all there is to it.' He sighed suddenly. 'Good God, can't you leave me in peace?'

Stahl did not seem to hear. He said: 'What if I tell you, too, that your wife Libertas has taken herself a lover – one of our guards. We don't mind. The poor woman is almost beside herself with fear, and the boy is handsome, a prime stud. He can comfort her in bed.' He looked down at the Major to check his reaction.

Schulze-Boysen sneered up at him, showing the many gaps in his once excellent teeth. 'What a petty bourgeois you must be! Do you think such things ever worried me or Libertas? Good luck to her.'

'Yes,' Stahl agreed mildly, after a moment's silence. 'I suppose you are right. I can see the kind of man you are, Major. Nothing will shake you, will it?' He paused momentarily, and then said quite bluntly: 'You have won!'

Peipe heard the two torturers gasp with shocked surprise. 'You can't mean that, Chief,' Fortner began, but Stahl silenced him with a flash of his eyes.

'There is only one thing, Major,' Stahl went on.

'Yes?' Schulze-Boysen's battered face showed hope, but his voice was still wary.

'You know whatever you say or don't say, you will be executed as a self-confessed spy.'

The prisoner nodded.

'Moreover the other eleven main accused will also be executed, including your wife.' Stahl made a chopping movement with his right hand, bringing it down on the palm of his other hand with a loud thwack like the sound of the executioner's axe hitting soft flesh. 'Now in spite of the fact that you worked for the Reds you are a gentleman of principles and of good family, I can see that.'

'Get on with it,' Schulze-Boysen snapped. 'Cut out the crap. What do you want?'

Stahl leaned forward. 'You might be able to save their lives if you were prepared to be co-operative, Major.'

Schulze-Boysen groaned. 'So you are starting all over again! Haven't I said over and over again, I know nothing about the resident in Belgium.' He rose to his feet groggily; he was a head taller than the policeman. 'All right,' he said, his voice very firm now, 'I shall make a deal with you. I've had enough of this farce.'

Stahl's sick leathery face lit up. 'Go on,' he said eagerly.

'I have certain documents,' Schulze-Boysen commenced slowly. Stahl's smile vanished. There was a pause, then Schulze-Boysen went on: 'Which would compromise the most prominent people in this rotten state if they were ever made public. There is no person, including the Führer, and no action which is left out of them. The world doesn't know the half of what goes on in your own hell-holes of concentration camps, for instance.' Schulze-Boysen played his trump card with all the deliberation of a professional gambler, intent on winning the pile at the end of a long session of gambling. 'This is my deal. Hitler will have lost the war by December 1942, and we will be freed if we live that long. If, therefore, I reveal where I have hidden those papers in Sweden, with the instruction that they are to be published when I die, will you agree to stay the executions 'till that date?'

Stahl gasped. The bastard had had this card up his sleeve all the time; that was why he had been so steadfast in the face of all the torture.

Peipe, watching the strange scene, could guess what was going through Stahl's head now. Stahl knew his bosses and their weaknesses: their perversions, their corruptions, their fears. After all, National Socialist Germany had always posed as a pillar of moral rectitude in the face of general European decadence. Hitler, Goering, Himmler and the rest, would never dare to have the details of their murky past revealed in the neutral press. It would be a serious political blow to them.

'All right,' Stahl cried through gritted teeth, 'all right, you bastard, you've got me by the short and curlies.' He swung round to face a shocked Fortner and Bass. 'For God's sake, don't just stand there like farts in a trance – get the big bastard out of my sight. *At once!*'

CHAPTER FOUR

For a whole week the interrogation of the 'Red Orchestra' prisoners (as they were now known in Prinzalbrechtstrasse) stopped, while the news of Schulze-Boysen's disclosure went from Ministry to Ministry and high official to high official, with Stahl fuming with impatience, waiting for someone to make a decision.

'Gestapo' Mueller, his chief, refused to make it. 'It's too big for me, Stahl. You ought to know that,' he growled in his thick Bavarian accent.

At the end of the first week, the Gestapo's representative at the German legation in Sweden reported that Schulze-Boysen had indeed spent a week's leave in Stockholm in the summer of 1939. His report added fuel to the fire of speculation and fear. Now the 'Stockholm Documents', as they were being called, hung over the Nazi Party, not like the sword of Damocles, but an obscene pail of blood and excrement.

'All I have to do,' Schulze-Boysen had confided to his cell-mate, who naturally was a Gestapo spy, 'is to press the button in Sweden and they'll publish. Then we'll see the sick look on the faces of those fat, self-important peasants. They'll shit their breeches with fear and shame!'

Goering ordered a total security clamp down on the subject of the 'Red Orchestra'. The affair was classified as a 'state secret'. Anyone merely talking about the traitors, and the hold they apparently had over the Reich's top officials, was liable to a death sentence. Swiftly it was given out in the Air Ministry that Major Schulze-Boysen was on an extended trip abroad. At the Economics Ministry, the Minister was informed his deputy Harnack had been taken seriously ill. The Minister sent flowers.

But still the rumours flourished in the anterooms of the Ministries and the darker corridors of the military headquarters. A myth took shape, and the wildest suspicions grew and grew. Admiral Canaris, Peipe's chief, was reputed to have said: 'This Red Orchestra network has cost us the lives of two hundred thousand soldiers.' Goering, the most seriously compromised 'self-important peasant' with his debauchery and drug-taking, was reported to have gone into hiding. Ribbentrop, the Foreign Minister, was reputedly asking for Goering's court-martial because he had been the man who had introduced Schulze-Boysen into the Air Ministry. Accusations and counter-accusations flew back and forth between the Ministries. As Stahl, nervous, impatient, now drinking two bottles of cognac a day, commented cynically to Peipe: 'If this goes on much longer, we'll have the brown bastards fighting duels with each other in the Tiergarten Park soon.'

Finally, it was Party Secretary Bormann who took the bull by the horns. The 'Brown Mole', as he was called behind his back in the Führer's HQ, deliberated a full forty-eight hours before he decided he would break the news to the Führer. As with everything he did, the squat, pudding-faced Bormann, who looked like a welterweight boxer who had gone badly to seed, planned the disclosure thoroughly. He waited until the Führer had eaten his frugal evening meal and was drinking his usual peppermint tea, flanked by his military cronies, the wooden-faced, stupid Keitel and the cunning, deathly pale Jodl, before he said almost casually: 'It appears that they are having some difficulty with those Red traitors in Berlin, *mein Führer*.'

'Trouble?' the most powerful man in Europe echoed the word. Then, as Bormann had anticipated, the Führer went off on one of his harangues, as was his wont at this, the most relaxed, part of his wartime day. 'Spies nowadays are recruited from two classes of society – the so-called upper-classes and the proletariat. The middle-classes are too serious-minded to indulge in such activity.'

Keitel, the inevitable toady, muttered his agreement, while Bormann waited to make his next move.

'Now the most efficient way of combating espionage is to convince those who are tempted to dabble in it that, if they are caught, they will most certainly lose their lives.' Hitler finished his peppermint tea with a flourish.

'Most certainly, *mein Führer*, only the most rigorous measures will succeed in rooting out this Red abcess in our body politic,' Bormann agreed. 'However, that bunch of traitors are from the so-called upper-classes, and they do know a great deal about important people in our state.'

'What do you mean, Bormann?' Hitler asked, shooting the

Secretary a sharp look. This time he was really listening.

Bormann swallowed hard. It was now or never! He licked his thick lips and plunged into the story of the 'Stockholm Documents'.

When he had finished, there was a dead silence in the plain wooden dining-room, with no sound save the steady tramp of the sentries' boots and the soft pad-pad of their guard-dogs on the gravel outside. Keitel, Jodl, Bormann and the rest, tensed for the storm that must surely come at the revelation. At such moments the Führer was unpredictable: the highest-ranking officers could be dismissed their posts, officials of top status could be sent into exile; heads invariably rolled.

To Bormann's surprise and relief, nothing of the sort happened. Instead, the Führer smiled mildly at the group, showing his yellowed, worn-down teeth. 'How simple you are, Bormann,' he commented gently. 'Like some naïve pastor's daughter from the backwoods. Make an agreement with the traitor and then, once you have the documents, *revoke it*! One does not honour agreements made under duress, especially when they are made with rats like that, who have the blood of German soldiers on their dirty paws.'

'Of course,' Bormann said. 'Why didn't I think of that, *mein Führer*?'

'Because you have the soul of a corner-shop grocer, Bormann, that is why. You – the lot of you – think in terms of honour and chivalry which belong in the nineteenth century. National Socialist Germany is engaged in a total war, fighting for survival. It has no time for such nineteenth century luxuries.' Hitler's voice rose and his dark eyes flashed fire. 'Get the documents at once. Then I want the whole dirty affair ended immediately.' He poked the air with his forefinger, a favourite gesture. 'There will be no more interrogations. Everyone knows they are spies. I want the bunch of them tried, found guilty, and executed as soon as possible. That is my final word on the subject.'

He rose to his feet: the evening meal was over. 'Now, gentlemen, to the map room. We must take another look at the situation on the Leningrad Front . . .'

He stalked out, leaving Bormann to his thoughts.

CHAPTER FIVE

'So we've got the word,' 'Gestapo' Mueller said in disgust.

Stahl looked across at his boss, with his drooping eyelids and square peasant face, in alarm. 'You don't mean you're going to stop the interrogation?'

'Of course, Stahl.'

'But Chief, there are much bigger fishes than the Schulze-Boysen lot to be caught still. And we can't net them unless we work more on that bastard of a major.'

'Gestapo' Mueller shook his head. 'There's not a chance of that, Stahl. You know the saying, "the Führer commands, we obey." Well, the Führer has commanded. No more interrogations. We're going to start trying them tomorrow.'

'But what about the pianist, and the resident in Belgium?' Stahl protested.

'Gestapo' Mueller shrugged carelessly. 'That's your problem, Stahl.'

Sadly, Stahl rose. He knew there was nothing more he could do. He and Peipe would have to start right at the damn beginning again.

Peipe and Stahl could hear the sound of hammering as they walked across the grey cobbled courtyard of Ploetzensee prison, where the trial was to begin that morning. Peipe looked curiously at the Gestapo man.

Stahl, still depressed by his failure with Schulze-Boysen, mumbled: 'The gallows – they're building the gallows for them.'

'Already? But they haven't even been tried yet.'

'It's all a stupid farce, Peipe, you must know that. They'll chop off their turnips as sure as tomorrow follows today. Come on.'

The accused stood up to the cross-examination carried out by *Obergerichtsrat* Manfred Roeder, the fanatical prosecutor, known to Peipe and all the legal profession as 'Hitler's Bloodhound', well enough – all except Libertas Schulze-Boysen. She had turned state witness, hoping that by doing so she might escape the death penalty. She was also desperately trying to get herself pregnant by the handsome young SS guard, for she knew that under German law a pregnant woman could not be executed.

Roeder lived up to his ferocious reputation as a fanatical Nazi. All the accused had confessed to spying. Thus for him they were already dead. Now he was more concerned to destroy their names and reputation for posterity; he didn't want them to live on as martyrs for the Communist cause.

He told the court how Schulze-Boysen had embezzled his organisation's funds; how his parties ended invariably in orgies; how he himself had indulged in homosexual affairs. Stahl, his leathery face set in a look of complete boredom at Roeder's bitter histrionics, whispered to Peipe, 'So what? As far as we of the Gestapo are concerned he could have fucked a pig. It wouldn't shake us. We know it all.'

'He's trying to destroy their reputation for posterity,' Peipe whispered back.

'Posterity doesn't take orders from a court-martial, especially one like this,' Stahl snorted.

Two days later, the court pronounced the verdict. All of them took the death sentence well, save Libertas. She screamed and fainted when the judges announced she was to be executed with the rest.

'So that's that,' Stahl announced wearily as they walked into the grey courtyard. 'Now we're back right to square one. You'll have to go back to Brussels.'

Peipe, depressed beyond measure, nodded. 'I'll start back on Monday. God what a life!'

'That, you can say again,' Stahl agreed. 'I'll be glad when it's all over and I'm safely tucked in my wooden box watching the potatoes grow from underneath. Good night.'

But Captain Peipe had one more duty to perform in the 'Red Orchestra' affair before he could leave to resume the hunt for the new pianist. On Sunday, Stahl, who looked worse than Peipe had ever seen him, gave Peipe a letter written on prison paper.

'Schulze-Boysen's last letter to his family,' he explained. 'You'd better have a look through it before we send it on. There might be a faint chance he's put something into it that could be useful.'

Peipe accepted the letter unwillingly.

'Oh, this also came for you – from Brussels.'

Peipe threw a quick glance at the handwriting. It was from Jeanette. He thrust it into his pocket.

Five minutes later, with the rain beating furiously at the window of his quarters, he began to read the condemned man's last letter.

It was addressed to Schulze-Boysen's parents and read: 'So the time has come; another few hours and I shall be parting company with my "self". I am perfectly calm and I beg you to be so, too, accept the news unperturbed. Such important things are now at stake on this earth that the extinction of a single human life is of small account.

'I do not wish to say anything further about what is past and what I have done. Everything I have done, I have done with the full knowledge of my heart and head, and by conviction. That is the light in which you, my parents, must accept them. I beg you to do so. This way of dying suits me. Somehow I always knew it would be like this. It is, in Rilke's phrase, my "personal way of dying".'

Peipe, moved strongly, forced himself to read the words for hidden meanings. But his heart wasn't in it. This man who was about to die was obviously above such pettiness.

He came to the last paragraph: 'If you were here – you *are* here, even if invisible – you would see me laughing in the face of death. I conquered my fear of it long ago. In Europe, blood usually has to nourish ideas. It is possible that we were only a pack of fools. But when death is so close, one is surely entitled to a little self-delusion. Now I reach out my hand to you all, and in a little while I shall deposit a tear here (just one) as a seal and as a token of my love.

Your Harro.'

For a long while, with the rain beating against the window the only sound, Peipe sat there with the letter in his hand, seeing nothing, hearing nothing. Finally he folded the cheap, yellow war-time paper very carefully, and deposited it in the official envelope, with its monstrous black eagle-and-swastika seal. He told himself he would post it personally; the dead man's parents had to have something.

It was only then that he remembered Jeanette's letter. He ripped open the envelope and let his gaze run along the scrawl. It was the usual emotional female rubbish. 'Love . . . I miss you . . . When are you coming back . . .' She seemed to repeat the same three phrases over and over again. In essence she said nothing, expressing only her need for him.

A little angrily he crumpled it and dropped it onto the table; there would be time enough for Jeanette when he returned to the Belgian capital. He put on his heavy leather coat, and placing Harro Schulze-Boysen's letter carefully in an inside pocket, he went out into the pouring rain, which, it seemed to him, was a suitable kind of weather for the tragic events of this day.

It was only much later that he remembered Jeanette's letter and asked himself how in the name of God she had known he was in Berlin, not to mention his address. *How . . .?*

THREE: A NEW CONCERT BEGINS

From: C
To: Wily
Subject: Suspect.
He is our man all right. See enclosed 'potted' biography. Ascertain the ramifications and extent of the organisation. Report via usual channels. Further orders will be given in due course. Good hunting!

C.

The young man sniffed. C's style was straight out of Whitehall. Not an ounce of feeling in it, except that upper-class 'good-hunting' at the end. 'Christ, if he only knew!' he muttered to himself in English, then, lighting a *Boule Nationale*, he settled back to read the document.

'From the description, etc., supplied by source, the suspect would appear to be Leopold Trepper, Jew, born in 1904 in Neumarkt near Zakopane, Poland.

'After the first world war he studied (according to Free Polish Intelligence) at the University of Cracow, but because of lack of funds, he had to give up his studies. From that time (estimated to be 1924) Trepper took a series of manual jobs until he took part in the revolt of the Dombrova Foundry workers. He was arrested and was sentenced to eight months in jail.

'It is supposed that during his period in jail Trepper became a member of the illegal Polish Communist Party. Adopting the cover-name of "Domb" (from the first four letters of the town of Dombrova), Trepper sought to enter France. His application for a visa was refused.

'In the end he managed to convince the Zionist but anti-Communist Hechalutz Organisation to smuggle him into Palestine illegally (source F.B.I.). By 1929, it is confidently reported by the Palestine Police, Trepper alias Domb was a member of the Central Committee of the Palestinian Communist Party and an organiser of the illegal Unity Group, which tried to unite Jew and Arab in the fight against the British Mandate Authorities.

'In 1930 Trepper, alias Domb, was arrested by the British authorities and after a short spell in jail, he effected an illegal entry into France (source Free French Intelligence). For some time he worked as a casual labourer in Marseilles until he became one of the Soviet Union's *rabcors*, i.e. a worker-correspondent, who passed on odd scraps of information to the legal Russian *rezident* in their Paris embassy.

'In 1932, the Russian *rabcors* system was cracked by the French police and Trepper just managed to escape, reaching Berlin, where he reported to the Russian Embassy. They sent him to Moscow. Trepper, alias Domb, had been sent back to school – the Russian espionage university.

'Nothing is known of his next six years.

'In 1938 Trepper arrived in Belgium bearing a Canadian passport, No. 43671 . . .'

The reader shook his head at such bureaucratic attention to detail. 'Christ,' he said to himself, 'as if I'm interested in the sodding passport number!'

'. . . which belonged to Michael Dzumage, who had last been heard of the year before when he had gone to Spain to join the International Brigade (source Royal Canadian Mounted Police and Free Belgian Intelligence). Forged and changed to the the name of Adam Mikler, it served Trepper for the next year while he set up his network in Belgium (we have no information from the Free Netherlands Intelligence on the network in Holland).

'After the Soviet–German friendship pact of 1939, it was the Soviet intention to ring the U.K. with a Russian network. As pre-war Belgian law was exceptionally easy-going on spies, punishing their activities only if these were directed against Belgian interests, Trepper, alias, Mikler, obviously found it an ideal base, using seven major seaports – believed to be Oslo, Stockholm, Copenhagen, Hamburg, Wilhelmshaven, Ostend and Boulogne – trading with the U.K., to run in agents.

'However, it is believed that by late 1940, Trepper, alias Mikler, began to urge his director in the Moscow Centre to turn the network against Germany. Obviously one year later the Soviet Union directed him to conduct all his operations against that country (M.I.5 reports no arrests of Soviet agents made after 1940). Apart from the Berlin ring, reported to us recently from "Source X" . . .'

The young man grinned. 'Source X,' he said softly. 'So that's how I'll go down in history.'

'. . . we have no further details of the network built up since 1940 by Trepper, alias Mikler.'

The young man's gaze fell on the note scrawled in green ink at the bottom of the page. It was obviously from 'C' –

he was the only one allowed to use green ink in the 'Old Firm'. It read: *'Watch him, Wily, he is a dangerous bastard.'*

CHAPTER ONE

On July 1st, 1942, Captain Peipe started to hunt the pianist and his master once again. Somehow the scent must be picked up again. While he concentrated on the nightly hunt for the music box, he asked the *Wehrmacht's* code experts to attempt to break the coded messages sent by the pianist. They might, he thought, offer him some clue to the damned pianist's location.

Peipe knew that if the encoded messages had been sent in French, English or German – and he suspected they would be one of those languages and not in Russian – the letters 'a' and 'e' would appear more frequently than – say 'x' or 'y'. A process of statistical examination would then show which letters had been substituted for these two most common letters. After that, it would be comparatively simple to deduce the rest of the coded messages.

But two weeks after Peipe had set the code-breakers to work, their chief in Berlin phoned him to say that the pianist was using a complicated grid system. 'I'm sorry, Peipe,' he said, 'but under this system over five thousand telegrams could be enciphered before any tell-tale repetitions. Naturally my boys will keep on working at it – they're so keen I'm having to give them a direct order to leave the office at night – but I'm afraid it might well take months before we get a break. Sorry, old chap.'

And that had been that. Peipe had realised that, now that he knew from Kranz that the pianist was operating in Brussels like his predecessor, he would have to commence the nightly slog through the blacked-out streets once again.

He requested the aid of the tracking teams once more. They arrived a few days later, and together with Fat Heinz and Peipe, they set off lugging their heavy suitcase-detectors up and down the silent, empty streets looking for their quarry.

But Peipe didn't get far. On the first night they had just reached the big black civilian Citroen, where Fat Heinz sat keeping radio contact with Kranz, for the second time to hear if Kranz had reported anything new which might help them, when a harsh voice said in German, '*Stehenbleiben!*'

Peipe turned, and was almost blinded by the bright beam of torchlight which was flashed directly into his face. He shaded his eyes with his one arm and saw two hard-faced military policemen standing in a doorway staring at him suspiciously.

'What are you four doing out at this time of night?' the taller of the two asked. 'Don't you know that there is a curfew?'

Peipe and the rest were dressed in civvies, and they all bore fake Belgian identity documents – the fewer people who knew what Peipe was up to in Brussels, the better – so he affected what he hoped was a foreign accent, and said in German, 'M'sieu, I know, but business – it doesn't wait for the curfew to be lifted, hein?'

'What kind of business?' the policeman rapped.

Peipe gave him what he hoped was a winning smile, the sort he had seen petty crooks give in the old days, and made the Belgian gesture of counting money with his thumb and finger.

'Black market, eh?' the policeman said.

'*Oui, M'sieu.*'

'All right, let's have a look at your identity cards – the lot of you.'

The two technicians looked uneasily at Peipe and then, putting their suitcase-detector in the back of the Citroen, reached for their papers. Carefully the two policemen scrutinised the four 'Belgians'' papers, and evidently found them in order. So they should, Peipe told himself, they were prepared by the *Abwehr's* leading 'shoemaker'.

But the two policemen were obviously not going to leave the matter there. Handing Peipe his ID card back, the taller one said, 'Black market, eh? Well, let's have a look in that suitcase there. We'll see what kind of horse-meat you bunch are flogging.'

Peipe knew that once they had seen the apparatus inside the suitcase, the story would be all over Brussels by the morning. No one gossipped as much as cops did; even if he ordered them to keep their mouths shut, they'd tell their superior officer who, undoubtedly, would pass it on to some other 'reliable chap' in the mess. No, he couldn't let them look at the case.

'Well,' the policeman grunted, 'are you going to open it? We haven't all night, you know.'

Peipe acted. He swung a punch at the big policeman. The blow caught him just below his chin strap. He slammed back against the wall. 'Quick,' Peipe yelled. 'Into the car!'

He sprang into the seat next to Fat Heinz, who reacted with surprising speed for such a gross man. In an instant he had started the motor, while the two technicians scrambled into the back. The big black Citroen shot forward. Behind them the two policemen unslung their rifles frantically. A volley of wild shots followed the crazily swaying car. Slugs howled off the walls on both sides. Lights started to go on everywhere. There was the shrill sound of a police whistle. Hoarse voices cried loudly in German and French. Next moment Heinz spotted a one-way street and went roaring up it, wildly scattering the cycle patrol which was hurrying to the two policemen's aid.

Ten minutes later they had parked safely and undetected outside the *Abwehr* office in the *Rue d'Anvers.*

'Phew,' Fat Heinz breathed a sigh of relief. 'They nearly had us by the eggs then, didn't they, Captain? What a balls-up!'

'That you can say again,' Peipe agreed wearily. 'All right, let's call it a night. We might as well get a few hours' sleep.'

But Captain Peipe was not fated to sleep much that particular night. Still a little angry at the night's fiasco, he opened his door to find Jeanette sitting in the living room's one armchair smoking morosely – and the heap of crushed, red-tipped butts told him she had been in his flat a long time.

'What the devil are you doing here at this time of night?' he demanded, both surprised and angry. 'And how did you know that I was back in Brussels . . .'

His words were drowned as she flung herself at him and crushed him to her breasts with a great passionate hug, pressing her hot, wet lips against his.

He pushed her away. 'Now Jeanette, it's nearly two o'clock in the morning . . .'

"Don't be angry with me, my sweet rabbit,' she interrupted, tears of sorrow and joy streaming down her silly pretty face. 'God, if you only knew how I've missed you all this time!' Her plump shoulders heaved violently and she started to sob broken-heartedly.

'All right, all right, Jeanette,' he said softly, patting her like he would a child. He no longer wanted to be loved after Lena; all the same he found the girl's pathetic, stupid devotion touching. He couldn't be angry with her. 'You mustn't get yourself worked up like this. It's not good for you.'

'But Horst, I thought you never were going to return,' she

said, looking up at him, her eyes swimming with tears. 'I couldn't bear it . . . and I've been bad, so bad, too.'

'You took a lover?'

That set her off sobbing again. He gave up asking questions. Instead he began to caress her breasts. It was the only way he knew how to comfort her.

One hour later she was snoring happily in his arms. She had come almost at once, with a tremendous frenzy of passion, and had fallen into a heavy contented sleep immediately. But in spite of his weariness, Peipe could not sleep. At the back of his mind, a little voice was beginning to ask awkward questions about the girl who now slept at his side. How had she known he had been in Berlin, and his address there? How had she known, too, that he was back in Brussels, when he had deliberately slipped into the Belgian capital on the midnight flight from Tempelhof, using the cover of the curfew to hide his return? Was it good guesswork on her part, female intuition – or something else?

He eased himself round and stared at her pale plump face in the silver light of the moon shining through the open window. It revealed nothing but child-like contentment. He bit his bottom lip thoughtfully. Was she more than she seemed, he asked himself, settling his head back on his pillow once more? Who was Jeanette really?

When he woke up next morning from a heavy drugged sleep, the sun was already high in the sky, and the room was unpleasantly warm and sticky with its rays. As was her custom, she was gone without having said good-bye. He looked across at the table where he stored his cigarettes. They were gone. As he had anticipated she had taken them – the lot. He sighed, and looked at the date on the calendar. March 31st, 1942. He would have to wait another three days for his next cigarette ration. But still, another month of this miserable existence was almost over. He rose and started to get dressed, preparing to face yet another day.

'Come to Pappa!' the new pianist said joyfully, as she came through the door. 'I've been waiting for this all month!'

He was lying full-length and completely naked on the bed, and it was very obvious that he was already excited and ready.

With a sigh, she started to take off her clothes. As she drew her dress over her head, his eyes caressed her plump young body greedily. He could hardly wait for her to remove her underclothes. Within five minutes it was all over, and he had not even made an attempt to make her come. All he had thought about was his own pleasure, the handsome young pig!

He lay there gasping fervently, so she started to pull on the frilly blood-red camiknickers that he liked her to wear, but when she tried to put on the matching bra, he opened his eyes and said: 'No, don't put it on. I want to see your tits.'

'Must you be so crude?' she asked, thinking of Horst, who was a real gentleman and cavalier of the old school, even with his trousers down.

'Well, if I can see them for a couple of minutes, the old machine will be ready for action again.' He tugged her little nipple idly. She winced with pain. The new pianist had done it without any real feeling. It hurt. But he didn't notice. He pulled out a packet of cigarettes, put one in his mouth and tossed one onto her red-silk covered lap. He lit his own, then threw her the box of matches.

'You really do treat me like a whore!' she said angrily.

'What's wrong with a whore, comrade?' he answered. 'Whores serve a useful purpose too, you know. They're also members of the great working class, even if they do work on their backs, with their legs in the air.'

'Can't you ever be serious?' she asked, lighting her cigarette.

'Life is too short to be taken seriously, someone who you don't know once said,' he answered, breathing out a stream of blue smoke gratefully. 'And by the way, we're all whores in this business, aren't we?'

For a moment she thought she detected a note of earnestness in his voice, as if this handsome casual young man, who seemed to have no depths as far as she could see, really meant what he said.

But his next question made her think she might well have been mistaken, for he asked in a bored manner: 'Seen the Big Cheese of late?'

'The *Grand Chef?*'

'The same.'

'No, not for a whole week. A courier brings the music notes for you. I don't think he's even in Brussels, or I would have heard from him.' she continued.

'Anything up?' he asked, running his big hand along the length of her silken thigh and penetrating between her legs.

She shuddered a little when his fingers found what they sought. It wasn't unpleasurable. Vaguely she hoped he would not come rushing on to her at once. She might come after all, then. 'I think it's that Berlin business. I have an idea that he's going to move the whole network somewhere else.' She wriggled as she felt his finger penetrate her.

'Where?' he asked.

She shrugged. 'Don't know.'

'Well, do you think we're going to stop in Belgium?' he persisted, beginning to move his finger energetically and not too inexpertly. 'I mean there is only Antwerp and perhaps Liège, big enough to hide a pianist in, away from the Boche detection vans.'

Her bottom lip fell open a little and tiny beads of sweat began to gather at the roots of her dark-blonde hair. She groaned pleasurably.

'I asked you a question,' he said.

'You ask too many questions,' she said with a gasp.

'I suppose I do. Must concentrate on the job at hand, eh, Jeanette?' he replied. 'All right, peel off those red drawers. I'm ready to go again.'

She cursed under her breath. She knew even before he put it in her that she wouldn't come . . .

CHAPTER TWO

Stahl flew in from Berlin two days later. Somewhat to Peipe's surprise, he had taken the *Abwehr* Captain's suspicions seriously enough to conduct the investigation himself.

'You were right to inform me, Peipe,' he said, as they sat together in the Brussels office, with a bottle of French cognac placed strategically at the Gestapo man's elbow. 'It is the logical thing for the other side to do. We did it ourselves with the Tommies in '39 in Holland, spotting every one who went into the Hague H.Q. of their Intelligence service and then posting an agent to watch the ones we suspected of working for them.' He took a drink of the Martell and smiled with pleasure. 'Like mother's milk,' he exclaimed, and continued. '*Abwehr* security is all right, I suppose, but it wouldn't take the other side too long to work out that your office doesn't seem to have any military function, like those of the rest of you base stallions.'

'Agreed. But of course it doesn't mean she has any connection with the Orchestra.'

'Naturally. She might have something to do with that bunch of crooks of the Witte Armee, the Belgian resistance movement. It's a regular part of their technique to attach – er – warm-hearted young ladies to likely German officers of the Occupation Forces.'

'Yes, I know. Jeanette's not too intelligent. I doubt if she ever got anything out of me,' Peipe said. 'She's hardly what you might call a Mata Hari.'

'I am sure you have been the epitome of discretion, my dear Peipe,' Stahl said quickly. 'Besides, you reported her yourself, and we'll keep the matter between ourselves anyway, so you have nothing to fear. Your reputation will remain unblemished.' He laughed at the serious look on the Captain's face. 'Your only problem will be finding yourself another skirt.'

'I wasn't worrying about myself. I was thinking about her. You must promise me you won't hurt her, Stahl.'

Stahl seized Peipe's one arm. 'Don't fear, old friend. I'm after bigger fish than your little whore. Once she's sung, we'll see that she's packed off to the provinces out of the way, in some cosy little cell for a couple of months. Then, if she is involved with the Orchestra, we'll quietly release her after the big fish are safely in the net. Never fear, your Jeanette will get out from under with only a black eye. Now, Captain, what about fixing me up with a bed in your quarters 'till the elusive M'selle Jeanette turns up again for another night of love and finds old Grandpa Stahl waiting for her . . .?'

She screamed when Stahl entered so unexpectedly from the bedroom. Instinctively Jeanette knew who he was. The ankle-length coat, the felt hat pulled down low over his leathery face and the cheap stub of an unlit cigar, stamped him for what he was.

'*Gestapo!*' she breathed, eyes full of fear.

Stahl touched his hat politely, took it off as an afterthought, and pulled out what he called his 'dog licence' – his metal identity badge. 'M'selle Jeanette Vandevelde?' he asked, quite formally, although he knew quite well who she was.

She nodded, too frightened to speak.

'I am afraid I must arrest you on a charge of espionage,' Stahl said in German.

To Peipe's astonishment, she replied in the same language. 'I didn't... I didn't want to do it – afterwards. But they forced me to continue ...' Her body was suddenly racked with sobs.

'But you speak German!' Peipe said. Both the girl and Stahl ignored him.

Stahl took off his coat, now that the formal part of the arrest was over, and taking Jeanette by the arm, guided her, still sobbing, to a chair.

'Now then, as I have already explained to Captain Peipe, you have nothing at all to fear if you co-operate with us. We're not after little fish like you. We're looking for the big 'uns. Help us to catch them and you're virtually a free woman.' He beamed down at her tear-stained face. 'You can take my word as a German officer that you'll be able to sit out any sentence you may receive on one cheek of your delightful little bottom. Now then, shall we begin?'

She looked first from Stahl to Peipe, who nodded winningly at her and then back to the Gestapo official. 'What do you want to know, please?' she asked in a small, broken voice.

'First things first. Tell me to what organisation you belong.'

She obviously misunderstood him, for she answered, 'The Belgian Communist Party.'

'No, not that, although you know it has been illegal since 1941. I mean, are you with the Resistance? Or something else?' he added very hopefully.

'We Communists do not co-operate with the Resistance,' she answered, as if she had learnt the words by heart at some agitprop meeting.

Stahl flashed Peipe a triumphant look. 'Then what exactly are you?'

'I was sent to observe Horst – Captain Peipe's – movements,' she said lamely, and then swinging round, cried fervently, 'But, Horst, you must believe me that when I picked you up in the *Bon Marché* that time, I didn't know I would fall in love with you. You must believe me, please!'

'Yes, yes,' he said hastily, hoping she wouldn't start crying again. 'I believe you, Jeanette. Just answer the questions.'

'And for whom were you to observe his movements?' Stahl continued in his hoarse voice.

'For the *Grand Chef*.'

'*Grand Chef?* Who's he, when he's at home?' Stahl asked quickly.

She shrugged. 'I don't know. Nobody knows. Most of us who work for him were introduced to him through the Party's Central Committee.'

'Then he doesn't belong to the Bělgian Communist Party?'

'No, and from his accent I'd say he's not even Belgian.'

'German?' Stahl snapped.

'He understands the language. But I don't think he's German . . . Somehow I don't think he's Western European at all. He's funny . . .' She broke off lamely, as if she couldn't put her thoughts into words.

'Describe him, please.'

She did so hesitantly, while Stahl made notes in a little black book which appeared from nowhere, breaking off every so often to fire a quick question at her. But she knew very little about the man, neither where he lived nor how he could be reached.

As Stahl concluded at the end of her explanation, 'Obviously our man's been around. He's a professional, one can see that. The way he arranged his *treffs* with the girl here shows he has been well trained. My guess is he's a Russian. He could well be the bloke those traitors in Berlin were reporting to.'

'Could be,' Peipe agreed. 'But first we've got to find him, Stahl, and from what Jeanette says, she has no means of contacting him and drawing him into a trap.'

'Agreed,' Stahl snapped, obviously very excited now at the thought that they were finally beginning to get close to the 'big fish', whom he took to be the Russian illegal resident for the Low Countries, if not for the whole of Western Europe. 'But there is one way we can collar him, Peipe.'

'How?'

'Through his courier to the pianist, and,' he turned his attention back to Jeanette again, 'you *do* know where the pianist is, don't you?'

She nodded numbly.

Peipe's heart leapt. They had him at last. 'Where is he, Jeanette?' he exclaimed. 'You must tell us.'

'But I can't . . . I can't betray him.' She dropped her gaze. 'He's my lover – and besides, you'd execute him if I told you.'

Stahl looked at Peipe and mouthed soundlessly the words: 'Somebody's been plugging the hole while you were away, old friend.' Peipe ignored him. He didn't care about Jeanette's love-life; he cared about finding the pianist.

'You *must* tell us, Jeanette!' he said. 'There is no other way. And listen, there is no need for the man to die.'

She looked up at him, new hope in her eyes. 'What do you mean? He's a spy, isn't he?'

'Yes, but you don't believe all spies die on the gallows? That fate is reserved only for the fools, and the ones who won't co-operate. If your pianist co-operates in – say – a radio game with his masters in Moscow, he won't have to die.'

'Radio game?' she queried.

'Yes, passing them misleading and fake information. Now, Jeanette, what's it going to be?'

She thought for what seemed a long time. Then she made her decision. 'Horst, you know I trust you.'

He nodded encouragingly.

'But the other gentleman,' she indicated Stahl. 'One has heard so much about the Gestapo.'

'All lies,' Stahl said hastily.

'But still I must make sure. I couldn't live with that man's death on my conscience. So this is what I will do . . .' she hesitated again.

'Go on,' Peipe encouraged her again.

'Tomorrow night when he starts sending again, I'll take you personally to his house. I must be present to ensure that he is not hurt. *Please!*'

Peipe looked inquiringly at Stahl. The other man nodded his head.

'All right, Jeanette, we agree to your condition. Is he armed?'

'No.'

'Good, then there is no danger to us or to you. Now, Jeanette, you'd better go and lie down in the bedroom. You can't leave here now 'til the raid tomorrow night.'

'Will you come, too?' she asked, brightening up now it was all over.

Stahl looked away, amused, and muttered something about sex having raised its ugly head once more.

'No,' Peipe snapped angrily. 'I have no time for such foolishnesses now, Jeanette . . . All right, Stahl, let's get on the phone and get this show on the road.'

CHAPTER THREE

It was a quiet evening in Brussels. Most of the city had fled the capital for the cool of the coastal resorts. Now the Germans had no intention of invading England, they allowed the civilians to return to the beaches and escape the oppressive August heat.

As the brazen ball of the sun started to sink below the roofs, housewives in dressing-gowns began to sprinkle water on the tired drooping flowers in their window boxes. Outside the cafes, the white-coated waiters were folding up the chairs. In the gutters the skinny-ribbed dogs gasped frantically for air, their tongues hanging out. It was the fag-end of a very hot day. Soon it would be dark and curfew would fall.

Stahl, standing in the doorway of the *Abwehr* office, looked with satisfaction at the truck-load of red-faced, sweating military policemen in full battle-order. They would do the heavy stuff just in case the pianist and his comrades tried to shoot it out. Behind the truck, there was a little Opel Blitz with the experts from Berlin – the locksmith, the safe-cracker and the demolition man – just in case the pianist had booby-trapped the room from which he transmitted, or the music box.

Stahl turned to Peipe, who was waiting in the coolness of the dark corridor. 'My compliments, my dear Captain, you've thought of everything, except one thing.'

Peipe, holding a pale-faced Jeanette's hand, asked: 'And what is that?'

Stahl grinned, pleased with himself and the planning of the raid. 'My medicine. But don't worry, I have taken care of that myself.' He pulled a little silver flask from his hip pocket and took a deep pull. Nodding to the driver of the lead car to start his engine, he said: 'Come on, young lady, let's get it over with.'

Numbly Jeanette let herself be led out of the corridor, pulling her veil down over her pale face as she did so. Peipe had insisted she wear a veil. He didn't want some nosey neighbour of the pianist to recognise her during the raid and pass the word on to the Resistance. They knew only one penalty for traitors – death.

Behind the leading car, the truck driver had started his engine too. It sprang to life with a tremendous noise, and the air was abruptly filled with blue smoke and the stink of diesel. Gallantly, Stahl opened the door for the silent Jeanette. 'Please get in the front next to the driver, young lady,' he commanded. 'You're in charge now. You must lead.'

Her eyes, scared and sad beneath the veil, looked at Peipe.

He nodded and she got into the seat next to the driver. Stahl and Peipe slipped into the back.

The driver, a fat little corporal wearing glasses, slipped into first gear and asked, 'Which way, gracious Miss?'

Stahl looked at Peipe, amused. 'Must have been a waiter before the war,' he whispered. 'Gracious Miss indeed!'

Peipe did not reply. He was too keyed up. Tonight, after they had taken the pianist, he'd ask for fourteen days' leave, he told himself. It had been a long hunt and he was sick of Brussels. He would go to the mountains – perhaps Bavaria – and get away from it all.

In a strained voice, Jeanette whispered, 'First to Boulevard Adolphe Max.'

The polite fat corporal obviously knew Brussels well, for he said nothing more. Letting out the clutch, he drew away smoothly from the kerb. A second later the truck and the car with the experts followed.

At a steady forty kilometres an hour, they rolled down the almost empty streets. Here and there a worker or some lounger, the usual cheap cigarette glued to his bottom lip, stared at the Germans without interest. After eighteen months of occupation, the Belgians no longer saw the Germans. They knew *their* war was over. Now they let the Anglo-Americans get on with the war while they occupied themselves with the business of living.

Peipe patted the girl's shoulder reassuringly and, turning to Stahl said, 'You know the plan, Stahl. Once the girl identifies the house, we park in the next street and work our way in from the rear, through the yard or the garden if the house has one. Just in case they try the same trick the last pianist did, and attempt to escape over the roof, I've instructed the sergeant in charge of the policemen to throw a couple of smoke bombs into the windows of the top floor. That should keep any would-be escapers down on the ground floors.'

'Good idea,' Stahl agreed, taking another drink from his 'medicine' flask. 'I was at the sawbones yesterday. According to the quack I'm not going to be around much longer. I'd like to get the lot of them in the bag before I trot off to my eternal happy-hunting ground.'

Peipe looked at the emaciated, ashen-faced Gestapo man, as if he were seeing him for the very first time. 'I must say you take your own – well, you know – very philosophically, Stahl.'

Stahl smiled softly. 'The world isn't all that great, you know, my dear Captain. When you're nearly sixty and your teeth are gone as well as your ambitions, not to mention the fact that all the lead's gone out your pencil,' he tapped his inner thigh, 'there's not much reason for sticking around longer than necessary, eh?'

'Yes, I suppose you're right, Stahl,' Peipe answered thoughtfully.

They fell silent. Now the convoy was rumbling through the mean little streets which led to the main boulevard. Here there were more people about. Shapeless women in sabots, carried long loaves of bread clasped to their bosoms; there were men in checked caps with scarves knotted around their skinny necks, and children, barefoot and dirty-faced, played tired games in the dust. Twice the fat corporal had to brake hard when children ran into the road following a ball. In the end he was forced to slow down and crawl through the streets in second gear. 'Damn kids,' he muttered, and then remembering he was in the company of a lady, he added: 'Please forgive my language, gracious Miss.'

Jeanette did not seem to hear. She stared moodily ahead into the deepening purple dusk.

They crawled on. Now they were nearly at the main boulevard. Stahl leaned forward and tapped Jeanette on the shoulder. 'When we're there, which direction . . .?'

In that instant the driver hit the brakes and the car shuddered to a halt, drowning Stahl's words and sending him banging against the front seat.

'What the hell–' Peipe began, as his startled gaze took in the steel drum which had rolled abruptly from nowhere right into the centre of the cobbled street, and forced the fat corporal to brake so sharply. His voice rose in a cry of alarm. 'Get down! It's a trap! *Duck!*'

Suddenly there were skinny little men with their hats pulled well down over their faces in the doorways on both sides, submachine guns in their hands. Just as Peipe and Stahl tumbled in a confused heap to the bottom of the car, the *Abwehr* Captain caught a last glimpse of the closest ambusher opening fire, his left hand resting on the air-cooled barrel, keeping it low as he scythed the gun from right to left. Then Peipe's world became a chaos of harsh, metallic, lethal noise, which drowned out the screams of the wounded and dying. The fat driver was flung back against his seat, his face split open, a bullet through his mouth. To his right the windscreen shattered into a crazy spider's web. Jeanette vanished. Slugs whined off the car. Behind them the policemen were flinging themselves over the sides of the trucks onto the cobbles, firing as they fell. Here and there a policeman yelped with pain as he was hit, and crashed to the ground. The ambushers kept firing and firing. White smoke was already beginning to rise from the Citroen's riddled bonnet. In a minute or two, the engine would catch fire, Peipe knew. But there was nothing he could do about it. They were pinned down by the hail of fire. The ambushers had picked an ideal spot. The convoy could go neither forward nor backwards.

Suddenly the sergeant in charge of the MPs, many lying on the ground, while their comrades cowered in the doorways, hugging what cover they could find and snapping off wild, inaccurate shots at the ambushers, acted. Completely ignoring the slugs which slapped the cobbles all around him, he doubled forward, overcome by rage and a sudden madness. Halting next to the wrecked, smoking Citroen, he raised the object which he held in his right hand. In the same instant that the burst of fire ripped open his chest and flung him against the wall as if he had been punched by a gigantic fist, the smoke-bomb exploded right in front of the ambushers. Thick white smoke billowed immediately into the dark purple of the sky. In a flash the ambushers couldn't see their targets. Their fire ebbed away, and finally stopped altogether.

Lying in a heap on the pavement, blood spurting from a dozen wounds across his broad chest, the sergeant called hoarsely: 'On yer feet ... on yer feet. Come on now ...' He slumped to the pavement, dead, just as the first of the MPs ventured into the street and began to advance on the men hidden now by a thick white mist.

Peipe slapped Stahl. 'Are you all right?' he shouted, above the fresh burst of fire.

'Yes . . . yes.'

'Let's get out of here!' Peipe wrinkled his nose at the stink of escaping petrol. 'The car's going to go up in flames at any moment!' Stahl needed no urging. He flung open the bullet-riddled door and dropped out. He grabbed the handle of the driver's door and pulled it open. The fat corporal's face looked as if someone had flung a handful of strawberry jam at it. 'He won't be serving any coffee and cake on the *Kudamm** any more, Peipe,' he yelled above the snap and crackle of the fire-fight and the sound of running feet as their ambushers started to escape.

Peipe was not listening. He was staring down at Jeanette,

* Fashionable street in Berlin.

whom he dragged out of the car to the safety of the nearest doorway. Stahl, his skinny body bent low, doubled across to him with surprising speed for a man of his age and condition. Stahl looked at Peipe and then at the girl. Her face under the absurd veil was ashen. A bullet had caught her in the centre of the forehead. A small neat hole, its edges were barely touched with pink.

He bent down, and raising her head gently to him, he held the glass of his big wrist-watch close to her colourless lips. The glass stayed clear. She was no longer breathing. Carefully he turned her head. There was a gaping wound at the back, almost as big as his fist, where the bullet had come out. Tenderly, very tenderly for him, he lowered her head to the pavement again. 'Poor cow,' he said, meaning it, 'she's bought it.'

'She didn't deserve it,' Peipe said numbly. 'She was a woman first, and then a spy – and a poor one at that.'

'Poor dead cow,' was all that Stahl said.

CHAPTER FOUR

'They were professionals, that's for sure,' Stahl said for the second time, and took another drink from his flask. Outside the cafe in which they sat, the ambulance sirens were howling, as they came and went, bearing away the casualties to the German military hospital. At the back of the cafe, a sweating young doctor, the back of his white shirt black with sweat, was cutting into the windpipe of a MP who had been shot in the mouth and was choking to death. Two burly comrades were exerting all their strength to hold him down as he writhed and twisted with pain on the blood-stained billiard table.

'Great crap on the Christmas Tree,' the young doctor was saying angrily, 'Can't you hold the bastard still? I'll slit his shitty throat in a minute, if you don't.'

Stahl handed Peipe his flask and said, 'Better have a drink. It'll do you good.'

Peipe took a drink and choked a little at the fiery spirit. 'Thanks,' he said. 'I've left you a drop.' He wiped the back of his hand across his cracked lips. 'What now?'

'What indeed?' Stahl answered moodily, finishing off the rest of the cognac.

With his free hand, covered with blood, the harassed young doctor slapped the choking man across the face. 'Now just you keep still, you miserable arsehole,' he cried angrily. 'Or I'll let you croak on this table.'

'The bastards are real professionals,' Stahl said for the third time. 'Everybody watches everybody. Typical Red technique. They'd been watching her and us all the time.'

'Do you think the pianist has done a bunk?' Peipe asked miserably, feeling sorry for the dead girl and for himself; now he would be lonelier than ever. 'I mean they surely would reason that the girl hadn't told us everything. Otherwise they wouldn't have put in the ambush – a very risky business indeed – in order to stop us reaching the pianist.'

'You might be just right, there,' Stahl said thoughtfully, new resolve in his faded eyes. His voice rose. 'All right. Assuming that they risked their necks to prevent us nabbing their pianist, we can assume that he is still operational here.'

Peipe nodded his agreement.

'Then let's get on the trail before it grows too cold.'

'What trail?'

Instead of answering his question, Stahl asked one of his own. 'Peipe, do you know her address?'

'Yes,' Peipe answered.

'Good.' Stahl rose hurriedly to his feet. 'Come on, let's see if we can commandeer some wheels out there in that mess. We've got a lot of work to do this night.'

As they went out into the night, the young doctor dropped his bloody scalpel with a clatter to the floor and exclaimed angrily, 'And now the shit has gone and snuffed it on me! What a shitty life!'

The hunch-backed old crone of a concierge was not impressed by the sudden appearance of two German officers in her little glass hutch at the bottom of the dusty, smelly, dark stairs. Nor did Stahl's harsh announcement of his organisation, 'Gestapo', have the usual effect. She had been dealing with policemen for fifty years. They left her cold.

Swiftly Peipe explained in French they had come about M'selle Jeanette, while the crone plucked at the long black hairs which grew from the end of her pointed chin.

'That whore,' was the concierge's only comment.

Peipe suppressed his anger. 'How did you know she was a whore, Madame?'

'So she's dead,' the crone commented. In spite of her years, she had noted the use of the past tense. 'How did I know she was a whore?' She answered her own question. 'Didn't go to work,' she cackled, 'but had meat every day and new clothes every month. And what kind of underwear did she have on the line on wash-day? Black filth!' She shook her head. 'You didn't need to be clairvoyant to see where she made her money – on her back with her legs in the air.'

Stahl looked at Peipe and shook his head in amused amazement. Then he said: 'And do you know where she went every day, you dirty old bag?'

Peipe translated the question for him, leaving out the 'old bag'.

'She took a tram every day. But where, I wouldn't know. How should I? I'm not nosey, you know.'

'Oh yes, I bet you're not nosey – not you,' Stahl commented, when Peipe had translated her answer. 'Now what?' he asked the *Abwehr* Captain.

'But I can tell you one thing,' the old woman said, before Peipe could reply.

'What?' he asked.

'She always rode for five francs, because every day she pestered me for change for a twenty-franc note. Those bastard Flemings who run the trams never want to change money for you. Though why she worried, I don't know. A quick feel of her ass and even a Fleming would have changed a note for her – with those tits!'

'That doesn't help us much,' Stahl said grumpily, when Peipe had finished interpreting.

'Oh yes it does,' Peipe countered. 'It tells us she took a tram daily within the five-franc zone. Come on, it's a start anyway,' He turned to the concierge and said, '*Merci et au 'voir, Madame.*'

The crone pulled another black hair from her pointed chin and grunted, 'They all come to a bad end. If you're born ugly like me, you always live to grow old.'

'That you can say again,' was Peipe's answer.

'All right,' Peipe ordered. 'Stop here, Heinz. This is the end of the five-franc zone.'

Obediently the fat sergeant drew up at the kerb while the two officers in the back stared out at the maze of shabby red-brick houses which made up the Brussels' surburb of Etterbeek. 'What now, gentlemen?' he asked, when neither of the two spoke.

'What indeed you fat rogue?' Peipe commented, depressed by the immense task in front of them. 'It will be like finding a needle in a damned haystack.'

'Now, let's look at it logically,' Stahl said thoughtfully. 'Let's start eradicating the places where the pianist could *not* operate.'

'The shops for instance,' the fat sergeant said. 'They couldn't use them at night. Neighbours would talk if they began to see shop-owners going in and out after normal hours.'

'Right,' Peipe agreed. 'But there are still a devil of a lot of houses left, even if you cut out the shops.'

'But there are houses and houses,' Stahl said thoughtfully.

'What do you mean?' Peipe asked.

Stahl took a drink of his 'medicine' from his flask before answering. 'You know the resident of any ring must always work a bit like a fiction writer. He selects his agents – like a pen-pusher selects his characters – and guides their actions carefully. Now if a novelist doesn't want the critics to slang him, he must work out a logical plot and make his characters act in a way compatible with the emotional and mental outlook he has given them.'

Peipe nodded and said, 'Don't make this too long, Stahl. We haven't got all the time in the world, you know.'

'Now just like the writer's characters, the resident's agents must live and work according to the role he has assigned them, unless they soon want to find themselves looking down the wrong end of a rifle barrel. So now to our houses. All those small one-family houses are out of the question. Put in an agent, in particular a pianist, who works all night and sleeps all day, and neighbours soon start asking what the man does for a living, why he doesn't got to work like normal working-class folk.'

Peipe's face began to lighten. 'I get your point, Stahl. So our pianist would have to disappear in order to work without question.'

'Right,' Stahl said. 'Into an apartment block where nobody knows his neighbour or wants to know him, where there's all sorts of types coming and going at any time of the day or night. So now you see what I mean, my dear Captain, about there being houses and houses?'

'I certainly do,' Peipe answered with alacrity. 'Heinz, get on that radio. I want a company of MPs and the radio detector boys.'

Heinz gave a mock groan. 'Not again, sir! Think of my feet . . .'

Two days after Jeanette's death, Stahl and Peipe came to the conclusion that the pianist might well be the occupant of one of three blocks of flats in Etterbeek. Peipe persuaded the *Luftwaffe* to lend him a Fieseler Storch, and together with one of the radio-detection team, he ordered the pilot to fly over the area of the three blocks on the third night. But although the light observation plane flew back and forth, until its fuel was almost gone, the radio-detection man's apparatus remained obstinately silent. The pianist was obviously not working.

On the fourth night, Peipe and Stahl led separate raids on two of the blocks. They turned up nothing, except six prostitutes and two deserters from the armed SS.

On the fifth night, the two officers and the company of police raided the last block. Peipe's plan was simple: to attack with brute force, working through the working-class tenement from the bottom floor to the top, which would be occupied immediately by a squad of MPs armed with flashlights, axes, even firemen's ladders in case the pianist managed to get on to the roof.

But the equipment was not needed. On the third floor, they struck lucky. According to the very scared male concierge, the right-hand flat on that floor was occupied by a young man, who never seemed to go to work and was visited regularly by a young woman – his fiancée, the concierge thought – who (from his description) could have been no one else but Jeanette.

'And where is the young fellow now?' Peipe asked eagerly. 'Still in his apartment?'

The concierge shook his bald head. 'No, sir,' he replied. 'At least I don't think so, because he hasn't been down into the yard to empty his pail into the trash for the last three days. I would have seen him otherwise.'

Stahl gave a faint smile. 'These Belgie concierges,' he said. 'We could use the buggers in the Gestapo. They watch everything.'

Peipe had no time for chit-chat. 'Come on,' he said eagerly, drawing his pistol with his one hand. 'It's him all right. Let's have a look-see.'

The concierge was right. The pianist had vanished. The little cooking stove hadn't been used for days, and the bread in the cupboard was already turning green. It was just about then, when the two despondent officers had come to the conclusion that they had lost the unknown pianist yet again, that Fat Heinz, doing a routine check of the walls, tapping them carefully to ascertain whether any spot sounded hollow, found the hidden door.

With renewed hope, the three of them burst into the room, which was dimly lit by a red bulb. It was empty. But once Fat Heinz had fetched a better bulb so that they could see what it contained, they realised it was a shoemaker's paradise.

The simple wooden table in its centre was littered with the equipment a shoemaker needed for turning forged documents: blank German, French, Belgian identity cards, rubber stamps, official application forms, both German and Belgian, bottles filled with various kinds of ink.

Stahl dropped the stamp he was examining and said, 'Funny – to put a shoemaker and a pianist in together, Peipe. Besides, didn't that concierge mention only one young bloke?'

Peipe nodded. 'But this is funnier, Stahl.'

'What?'

Peipe handed him a dark blue French ID card. 'Take a look in that.'

Stahl flipped open the identity card with the practised ease of a cop who had examined many thousands of such documents in his time.

There were no particulars filled in on the right side. But on the left there was a photograph, already stamped with the seal of the Paris Prefecture. It depicted a heavy-faced, confident-looking man with dark-blond, cropped, wavy hair.

'Now,' Peipe said, after he had allowed the Gestapo man to look at the photograph of the unknown man. With his one hand, he tendered Stahl the waste-paper basket from under the wooden table. 'What do you make of that?'

It was half-full of what were obviously completed ID cards, which had been carefully shredded so that the particulars and photos of their intended recipients were completely destroyed.

Stahl whistled softly through his teeth. 'I see what you mean. Those all destroyed, and this one—' he tapped the French ID card '—left on the table for anyone to find. Very strange, my dear Peipe.'

'Very strange indeed, Stahl.' Peipe hesitated and looked directly at the Gestapo man. 'It almost seems as if the shoemaker wanted us to find the thing . . .'

FOUR:
THE CONCERT COMES FROM A NEW HALL

The young blond man took one last glimpse out of the dirty window at the concrete jungle of Menilmotant, and shuddered at what he saw. Hastily he pulled to the heavy velvet blackout curtains. His eyes did the usual check of the door. It was locked and bolted, and the chain was in place. Satisfied, he eased himself into his chair in front of the transmitter and slipped on the earphones. Despondently he stared at the luminous hands of the big alarm clock. Nearly eight o'clock. It would be dark by now – the days were getting shorter again – and curfew would be imposed. He could begin.

He clicked on the power and tuned the transmitter to 15,600 kilocycles, the frequency he employed on alternate nights when he signalled the Cheltenham receiving station. It was just on eight. He flashed a quick look at the long coded message to his right which had taken him most of the afternoon to encipher. All right.

Suddenly the alarm rang. It startled him, although he had set it himself. The strain was beginning to tell, he told himself, and clicked it off. Next instant his finger hit the morse buzzer and he started to transmit with the ease born of long practice.

'The organisation is spread throughout Occupied Europe. Trepper has agents in Holland, Belgium, France and apparently still in Germany, to judge from the material which is again passing through my hands for Moscow. It appears to come from military sources.

'Since our move, Trepper is obviously making France the centre of his operations. Here in Paris, he has at least six sources. There are also other agents reporting from Lyons, Marseilles and probably from Grenoble too.

'He has started a cover firm, named Simex, which is located in the Champs-Elysées just above the Lido.'

The blond young man smiled to himself and wondered what 'C' would make of the unnecessary reference to the Lido.

'The Simex undertaking is apparently a good idea. It supplies the Germans, in particular the Todt Organisation, with heavy materials, purchased on the French black market. As a result the Germans know the firm is operating illegally and presumably accept that Trepper and his employees are dubious characters – how dubious they little realise. In addition the Germans supply Simex and its operatives with the necessary documentation to be out after curfew, visit military installations on business, etc., etc. It is a perfect cover.

'To be brief, Trepper's organisation is still very healthy, well financed from the black market ops, and receiving important military and economic information to pass on to Moscow from varied sources.'

The young man hesitated for only a second; then he rapped out his last sentence. 'First evidence planted. Request further instructions?'

The next moment he had flipped the 'off' switch, pulled the plug out of the mains and sunk the transmitter into the old-fashioned, pre-war Singer treadle sewing-machine. He ran the bag of ice cubes he had already prepared across the top of the sewing table. A second later he felt the surface. It was quite cool. The ice had cooled the transmitter off.

Now he rose and went to the door. Carefully he undid the bolt, unlocked the door and released the chain. He glanced around the door. 'Damn,' he said to himself in English and then automatically corrected his slip by saying aloud '*merde*'. He had forgotten the coded message.

Swiftly he grabbed it, took it to the evil-smelling little lavatory. Carefully he set it alight with a match and watched it crumple into black charred nothingness in the bowl of the *bidet*, before finally flushing away the ash with a quick turn of the twin taps. Only then did he flop down on the still unmade bed. Greedily he grabbed a *Gaulloise* and lit it. As he did so, he noticed that his hand was trembling violently.

CHAPTER ONE

With a sigh of relief the driver of the cycle-taxi, which had brought Trepper to the hospital from Chrisy-le-Roi station, got down from his saddle and wiped the sweat off his forehead. 'That hill is a shit!' He panted heavily.

Trepper, clad in his black-market businessman's suit with the tiny ribbon of the *Légion d'Honneur*, which he hadn't been awarded, but which seemed to go with the suit, in the lapel, smiled understandingly. He reached in his pocket to pay, and added a twenty-franc tip.

'Thank you, sir,' the skinny driver of the cycle-taxi, whose bare legs were as muscular as any Chinese rickshawman's, said appreciatively.

'That's all right,' Trepper said, adjusting his homburg carefully. 'But remember to pick me up at the usual time.'

'I will that, sir,' the man said, and mounting his bike, he want sailing down the hill, obviously heading straight for the *Estaminet de la Gare.*

For a moment Trepper stared at the outside of Anna's 'Rest Home', her own name for the private lunatic asylum which she ran. It wasn't exactly a château. It lacked the usual towers and turrets. But it was definitely a distinguished, gracious building, set in a thick semi-circle of wood, which must once have belonged to some local aristocrat. At all events it fitted into the picture that Anna and Baron Vasili Maximov had created for themselves in right-wing French and German Army circles.

Picking up his smart briefcase from the gravel where the driver had deposited it, he opened the gate and walked in. But he didn't get far. His attention was caught by the loud bellow of a voice which would have done credit to a drill sergeant. He swung round. It was Anna – all three hundred pounds of her – her massive fists on her ample hips, shouting up at the patient almost hidden in the oak tree to her front.

'You naughty boy,' she called in her accented French. 'Now, you come down here at once and put your clothes on! You'll catch your death of cold.'

Something white glimmered in the tree. Trepper caught his breath. The patient – a big man in his thirties with a shock of black hair – was completely naked. With his right hand clasped to his lower body, he was making a very obscene gesture indeed.

Trepper stopped and wondered what Anna would do. The huge Russian woman wagged a finger like a sausage at the lunatic and bellowed, 'Now you are being very bad – do you understand – very bad. But I'm warning you. If you don't come down from that tree at once, I shall have to come up and get you.'

The lunatic made the same obscene gesture with his thumb and forefinger.

'Then that does it!' she bellowed. Rolling up the sleeves of her white coat to reveal two massive muscular forearms, she grabbed the tree trunk and started to shake it back and forth as if she might rip it out by the roots any moment.

Leaves came down like green rain. Twigs started to patter to the ground. Desperately, his sexual desires flown now, the naked man tried to retain his hold. Anna increased her shaking, her broad Slavic face lobster-red and sweating with the effort. Suddenly the branch the naked man was holding, broke off. Caught off his guard he fell to the ground, flat on his face in a pile of leaves. Anna sprang forward. Before he could struggle up, she had descended upon him, legs spread wide to reveal massive thighs above the tops of her black woollen stockings. Like a professional wrestler, she clamped a powerful half-nelson on the winded lunatic, crying, 'Now I've got you, you filthy boy! On your feet and back to your room. There I'm going to put you under a nice ice-cold shower. That will put all those nasty ideas out of your filthy head.'

The man groaned piteously as she jerked him to his feet, and holding him thus, she frog-marched him grimly back to the house, with Trepper following, a broad grin on his face.

Anna was tough. Often she had told him, with that Russian attention to detail, how as a young girl she had waited behind the door of their stately home with an axe in her hand while her father, Baron Maximov, a Tsarist general, had tried to find an escape route for the family from the advancing Red revolutionaries. From St Petersburg, where they had spent the first years of their lives in Imperial splendour, the two Maximovs, Anna and Vasili, had been faced with the prospect of making a living in Paris which swarmed with seedy White Russian refugees. But somehow they had made it, Vasili becoming an engineer, and Anna a doctor.

Up to 1941, the two of them had remained right-wing, anti-Communist Russians of the old school. But with the German invasion of Russia in 1941, the two emigrés had decided they were patriotic Russians first, Imperialists afterwards. They turned to the French Communist Party and asked how they might help the Russian cause, and in its turn the Party had contacted Trepper.

Trepper had been suspicious. After all Vasili was a Baron and the son of an Imperial general. He sent an urgent signal to the Moscow Centre for information and a decision. Moscow had advised him to hire the strange pair as Soviet agents, but to treat them with extreme caution.

To his own surprise, the two of them, especially Vasili, had turned out to be a great success and the mainstay of his operation in France. Anne opened her hospital with its spacious grounds and fine rooms to high-ranking German officers wanting to spend a weekend away from the capital. Vasili, on the other hand, had taken a job in Paris, and thanks to Anna's connnections he had managed to obtain a pass to the Hotel Majestic, which the Germans used as their G.H.Q. And it was here that he really struck lucky.

At forty-four, Vasili Maximov, with his skinny body, pinched face, and incongruously elephantine legs, was no Casanova. But somehow or other he had appeared Prince Charming himself to Magarete Hoffman-Scholz, a German lady of uncertain age, who had spent the last quarter of a century apparently waiting for a 'cavalier of the old school' (as she always described the skinny little Russian to her friends) to walk into her life.

But Fraulein Hoffman-Scholz was not just another elderly virginal spinster who had waited 'til it was almost too late to lose her innocence. She was the secretary to Colonel Kuprian of the German G.H.Q. and had an uncle, Colonel Hartog, who was on the staff of General Stulpnagel, the German Governor of *Gross-Paris*. With her contacts and background she was an excellent source of information about the German Army, and not long after Vasili had become her lover and had been admitted to the same circles, she was passing on anything he wanted to know.

Now on this fine autumn day, Trepper was making his usual weekly visit to see what the strange pair of agents had found out for him during the course of the last seven days. Anna, now recovered from her exertions with the naked man, was waiting for him in the big office. But as he knocked and entered she held her big forefinger to her unpainted lips in warning. Trepper followed the direction of her gaze, and saw the reason for her caution. Through the glass window of the office, he could see one of the German nurses attached to the hospital, looking at a file of papers in the next office. A minute later she had gone, and Anna said: 'You can't trust those grey mice. The Boche attach them to French hospitals as spies. They've got their ugly German eyes and ears everywhere.'

Trepper smiled. Anna was right. The grey mice, as they were called on account of the drab grey uniforms they wore, probably did function as part-time informers for the Gestapo. 'You're learning the tricks of the trade quickly, Anna. My compliments,' he said.

'After you've been dealing with crazy people most of your life, like I have, you learn to be on your toes all the time.

Otherwise God knows what dirty little tricks they'll play on you.'

Trepper sat down and said, 'Yes, so I notice. I saw you tackle that naked chap a little while back.'

'Oh him,' Anna said easily, opening a box of German cigars and after he had taken one, taking one herself. 'Exhibitionist. Always wanting to beat his meat in front of women. If he carries on like that much longer, 'I'll have to tie his hands behind his back.' She breathed out a cloud of blue smoke. 'Or perhaps I'll let him perform a couple of times in front of that little prude of a grey mouse. That'll frighten her off for good.'

Trepper nodded, and then got down to business. 'What do you have for me this week, Anna?' he asked. 'And please not so quick. I have to memorize the stuff, you know.'

Speaking slowly and deliberately, relating the information from memory herself, for he had warned her at the beginning of her new task that she must not take notes and put anything down on paper, she gave him the details of the divisions which were leaving France that autumn for the Eastern Front; the names of the two SS panzer divisions which were moving to Normandy for a refit after their battering in Russia; the means the Germans were going to use to solve their growing manpower problem in the *Reich's* factories – they were going to start conscripting Frenchmen; and other odd titbits of information that she had garnered from her own various sources.

Trepper tapped the ash off the German cigar. 'I am very pleased with you, Anna,' he said. 'The Centre will be exceedingly grateful for the information. The knowledge that two SS armoured divisions have been withdrawn is very useful in itself. It could well mean that the Germans are going over to the defensive again this winter. I am sure there is a medal in this for you.'

She shook her blond head, her massive bosom trembling violently under her white doctor's coat. 'I don't want a medal, Trepper. All I want is to do something for Mother Russia in her hour of need.'

'Don't we all, Anna,' Trepper, the Polish Jew, answered, tongue in cheek. 'Anything else?'

'Just gossip.'

'Gossip?' Trepper asked, his mind already on other things.

'Yes. Last weekend I had the honour of being the hostess to a select group of the General Staff – all beer bellies, fat arses and – by the look of them – nothing in their breeches.'

Trepper laughed at Anna's choice of words. She knew no inhibitions. 'And?' he prompted.

'Well, in front of me they don't curb their tongues. After all, I'm one of them. On Saturday night, after they had fed their faces and guzzled most of my best Hennessey, General von Pfeffer – you know, the one who signed the armistice with the French in 1940? – opened up. Too much cognac, I expect. Anyway, he said that, of course, he was delighted with the success of German arms against the Communist plague. But, in his opinion, the Reds could never be crushed as long as Germany was at war with England and America.'

'Go on.'

'Well, the pompous old asshole maintained that the Boche should start negotiating with the Tommies and Amis so that the whole weight of the *Wehrmacht* could be thrown against Russia.'

Trepper looked glum.

'Colonel Hartog – he's on the staff, too – asked "and what about the Führer?" To which Pfeffer said, "negotiate, with or *without* the Führer".' She stopped, and awaited Trepper's reaction.

It was unusually violent for him. 'The capitalist bastards!' he exploded. 'Now we've got them on the run, they're trying to save their own skins by turning to the English. But believe me, Anna, once we've seen off the Germans, we'll tackle them too – and the Americans.' He slammed his big fist onto the desk. 'One day, we Communists will rule the world . . .'

CHAPTER TWO

Trepper was pleased.

The round-up of his Berlin ring and the trouble in Brussels had been severe blows, but the new Parisian stronghold seemed to be both profitable and impregnable.

He had lookouts everywhere and they, together with his rigid internal security system, made the new ring proof against any Gestapo or *Abwehr* assault. With the money he made through the Simex operation from the Germans, not only could he finance half-a-dozen or more empty apartments in Paris for his agents – and naturally, the all-important pianist – but he could also bribe the German supply officers, with whom Simex did business, very liberally.

In a way it was ironic. The Third Reich was subsidizing his new Orchestra, just like a human body unknowingly nourishes the cancer which will finally kill it. Indeed, the Director had recently signalled him from the Moscow Centre that Stalin was considering making him the banker for the whole of the Western Operation, including the Soviet espionage ring in the U.S.A. and South America. It would be a great honour.

Now in this mild autumn of 1942, Trepper felt supremely confident. Simex had already penetrated the German Todt Organisation, the civilian labour force which did all the Wehrmacht's building for it; Vasili Maximov supplied him with what he wanted to know about High Command decision-making; and Anna's odd titbits about internal German politics were extremely useful.

In his own capacity as a wealthy businessman, who enjoyed the confidence of the Germans, and the crooks of the French black market, Trepper also had many sources of information, mostly supplied unwittingly during the course of long boozy lunches, or sometimes for money handed over by a third party – for Trepper was not going to take the risk of offering a bribe for information himself.

And in the final analysis, a whole army of Communist Frenchmen belonging to the Communist *Franc-Tireurs et Partisans*, the biggest Resistance movement, toiled unknowingly for the new Orchestra. Each time the Resistance men overran a German post or ambushed some lonely German truck-driver, his papers and what other documents they could snatch, were forwarded – through a complicated and infiltration-proof series of cut-outs – to Simex, for assessment and evaluation. Every time some brave female comrade allowed herself to be 'seduced' by some randy Boche in order to pick his brains, whatever she found out finally landed on Trepper's desk. And any time that some drunken German talked too much in some little *bistro*, the comrade waiter, who served the drunken soldier so humbly, would undoubtedly pass his besotted confidences and boasts on to the Simex network. Leopold Trepper, the son of a humble Polish Jewish pedlar, felt that he was running the strongest and most powerful spy Orchestra that the world had ever known. But in his pride he overlooked one thing. *If his organisation was impregnable to assault from outside, it was wide-open to attack from within.*

CHAPTER THREE

In the first weeks of that autumn, Peipe and Stahl, plus a small staff of *Abwehr* men and radio-detection experts, moved to Paris, setting up their headquarters in the old French Sûrete building in the Rue des Sausasies.

By now the code-breakers in Berlin had finally broken the Orchestra's code and were sending alarming reports on the breadth and depth of the messages being sent by the unknown pianist to Moscow. At the F.H.Q.* in East Prussia they were furious at such treachery, and it was stated by those who should know that the Führer was even considering having his own staff checked by the Gestapo, in case there was a traitor among them. As 'Gestapo' Mueller signalled Stahl: *'If you want to live to die a nice comfortable death in a warm bed, find and destroy that Orchestra – soon!'*

'Easier said than done,' Stahl had snorted to Peipe when he had received the signal. 'There are frogs and other foreigners working at every level of the *Wehrmacht* and the Todt Organisation, from the Army's brothels right up to the higher Headquarters. Any one of them, or *all* of them– as far as I'm concerned – could be passing on info to the damned Orchestra.' He sighed with exasperation. 'How in hell's name are we going to be able to check out some 50,000 Frenchmen and women? The Ivans will be on the Channel coast by then, and they'll be escorting Hitler through the streets of Moscow in a monkey's cage!'

Peipe had laughed at Stahl's angry outburst at the enormity of the task facing them, but after a couple of days in the French capital he had been forced to agree with the Gestapo man. The French as a nation had accepted the 1940 Armistice. Since then, most Frenchmen and women were concerned solely with how to procure the next meal. In the ancient open trams, the dingy little *bistros* and bars, the offices, the queues, they talked (or so it seemed to an attentive Peipe) of nothing but *food.*

Yet there were still two classes of people in Paris who didn't need to talk about food, for they could eat what and when they liked, because they had taken sides. On the one hand, there

* Führer's Headquarters,

were the political and economic collaborators, who had decided to work, directly or indirectly, with the occupying power. And there were plenty of them. The German offices everywhere were flooded with well-fed, smug men and women, who were prepared to go to any lengths to please their conquerors. On the other hand, there was another and smaller group, which had opted to fight against the conquerors. These men and women were debarred from normal sources of food, for they lived illegally with false names and false addresses. But they had plenty of money, supplied to them by a half-dozen Allied governments.

So it came about that in the discreet, but always overfilled, black-market restaurants around the *Gare de Lazare* and off the *Place de la Concorde*, collaborators, black marketeers and Resistance men rubbed shoulders with high-ranking German officers and their fur-clad French mistresses. All of them would one day pay the real bill for their junketting in wartime Paris while the rest of the nation starved – and they would pay it in blood. But in the autumn of 1942, that thought didn't help a frustrated Peipe very much.

He knew that the man he sought – the conductor of the Orchestra – would be found in one of the black-market restaurants. For all he knew he might well have already sat opposite the conductor in one of the many bars and restaurants in which he spent his days now.

As he explained his vague theory to Stahl: 'A fellow like that – the conductor, I mean – must have plenty of money to finance the Orchestra, and it must be a damned big Orchestra, to judge by the amount of radio traffic coming from his pianist.'

'Still no fix from the *Funkabwehr* boys?' Stahl had interjected.

Peipe had shaken his head quickly and continued, 'Now, to go along with your theory, Stahl, that the master-spy must be like a novelist – he must give himself and his people roles which are realistic within the given framework of a book or organisation – then our conductor must pose as a wealthy man.'

'Agreed. So our man must appear in the black-market restaurants and bars because that's what these fat cats of Parisians do, probably with some fancy whore on his arm.'

'Exactly,' Peipe had said. 'Now let's take it a little further, Stahl. What is he posing as and what group will he work with – our new allies the collaborators, or the gentlemen of the other side, the Resistance?'

'Well, certainly not the second group, Peipe. It is standard operating procedure with the Russians that they only have the most limited contact with the Party in whatever country an Orchestra is playing.'

'What about the other Resistance movements – De Gaulle's, or those financed by the Tommies?'

Stahl had pouted his bottom lip. 'Don't think so, Peipe. The Ivans don't like anybody looking at their cards. They prefer to play them close to their own hairy chests.'

'So you have probably come to the same conclusion that I have, Stahl,' Peipe had exclaimed eagerly. 'The role he is playing is that of a collaborator.'

'Exactly. Wouldn't it be the best means of getting in and out of these base stallions' offices and making the kind of high-level contacts with the *gentlemen officers*,' Stahl sneered at the words, 'who would supply him with the kind of info he needs? Besides, these collaborators are usually making a pile on the side and that fact would explain our conductor's wealth if anyone started asking awkward questions.'

'So,' Peipe had concluded, 'we are beginning to get a little closer to our man, aren't we, Stahl?'

'Are we?'

'Yes. We are looking for a wealthy collaborator who has widespread access to the German authorities, probably one of the kind you can see nightly in the Ritz, wining and dining important *Wehrmacht* quartermasters as if money were no object.'

'There must be hundreds, perhaps thousands of fat cats like that,' Stahl had grunted morosely.

Peipe's eyes had sparkled with excitement. With his one hand he took the pass out of his empty sleeve-cuff. 'You're forgetting one thing, my dear Inspector. We have a photograph.'

Thus while the beaten German armies, which had advanced so boldly into the Caucasus that spring, started the grim, bitter withdrawal to an obscure Russian industrial city on the River Volga, named Stalingrad, a copy of the photograph taken from the ID card seized in Ettelbeek, was circulated to every German office and organisation in Paris.

But as the weeks passed, and no one to whom the photograph had been circulated reported to Stahl and Peipe, the two of them began to lose hope in the success of the operation. As Stahl, who was obviously now going into the final stages of his dreadful disease and was drinking two bottles of cognac a day to deaden the ever-increasing pain, croaked to Peipe, 'There are two possibilities, Peipe. Either those of our people who might recognise the conductor are covering for him, out of loyalty,' he made the contemptuous gesture of money being counted with his thumb and forefinger, 'in other words, their silence has been bought, or—' he coughed thickly and a little trickle of pink blood appeared at the corner of his wizened mouth.

'Or?' Peipe asked in alarm.

'Or that damned photo was a plant, and it isn't the conductor at all. Now please pass me my medicine. I'm going to go off and get stinking.'

With that he had stamped drunkenly out of the Cafe Georges V on the Champs Elysées, black-market Martell clutched in his claw of a hand, leaving Peipe staring after him in a mood of black despair.

CHAPTER FOUR

It was Vasili Maximov who warned Trepper. They met, as was their wont, once a month, in the mental hospital at Choisy-le-Roi. In spite of the extra rations that his German mistress provided him with, the Russian Baron looked as skinny as ever, his face pinched.

'You don't exactly look as if you're thriving, Vasili,' Trepper commented in Russian, when Anna had gone to keep her eyes on the 'grey mice'. I must see that you get some more to eat, little brother.'

'*Boshe moi!*' Vasili answered in Russian too and slapped his skinny cheek. 'It's not the food, it's the demands the woman makes on me that makes me so skinny. I've not had a good night's sleep in weeks.'

Trepper laughed sympathetically, and said, 'Remember it is for Mother Russia, Vasili.'

'That I know, but there is more, dear friend.' He paused. 'Tongues are beginning to wag,' he added miserably.

'What do you mean?' Trepper asked, amused at the skinny little aristocrat's apparent misery.

'Unless my relationship with Margarete is placed on an official footing, there is undoubtedly going to be scandal.'

'Do you mean she wants you to marry her?'

'Yes, indeed. What a terrible prospect, don't you think? I mean – *that, every night!*'

'But my dear Vasili, you must,' Trepper urged, his amused look vanished now. 'Don't you realise that if there's a scandal, they might exclude you from official German circles? Then your usefulness as an agent would be null.'

'Have pity, Trepper,' Vasili pleaded, his pinched face contorted with misery. 'Can't we do it like this?' Swiftly the Baron explained that if he decided to get engaged to her, it would postpone the horrible prospect of marriage to the German woman for another few months. 'Sort of a second line of defence, Trepper . . . and thank heaven, in our circles engaged couples do not sleep together. I'll be able to get some rest at last.'

Trepper laughed sympathetically and clapped him on his skinny shoulder. 'Excellent, excellent, my dear Vasili, we'll make an agent out of you yet . . . Now listen, you're obviously accepted in Boche circles, but still you must be careful. Do nothing which will put you at the mercy of a routine police check.'

'What do you mean?' Vasili asked, obviously relieved now that the problem of marriage had been solved.

'Well, for instance, never carry that pistol I know you have; keep away from driving a car; always ensure your ID card is up to date. You know how it is. Once the cops start checking, they can turn up all sorts of things, especially those French flics working for the Boche. They are worse than the Germans themselves.'

'Agreed, agreed. But I'm careful, especially with the new man I told Anna to tell you about.'

Trepper leaned back in his chair. Somewhere one of Anna's patients was screaming his head off in a maniacal, animal manner which sent a slight shudder down the spymaster's spine. 'Oh yes, Vasili, I remember. Tell me more.'

'He's a Frenchman, but a patriot, who works in the *Wehrmacht's* Central Billeting Office in the capital. Now it's part of the job of his department to ensure that every Boche soldier has the chance of a few days' leave from the Front, in Paris. You know, the Follies and the ladies-of-joy in Pigalle.'

Trepper nodded his understanding. 'Go on.'

'Well, of course, the Boche can't send whole units to Paris, but individual soldiers are picked by ballot and moved to the capital, and it's our Frenchman's job to ensure that *Soldat* X coming from point B has a billet waiting for him when he reports in at the RTO* at the *Gare de L'Est.*'

Trepper's heavy dark face brightened. He saw immediately what Vasili was getting at. 'You mean your piffling little French clerk knows where every German unit at the Front is?' he demanded incredulously.

'Well, he knows where all those are which send men on leave to Paris – and that's most of them,' Vasili answered proudly.

'In the name of the Black Virgin of Kazan!' Trepper exclaimed. 'The man's a treasure. With the aid of a chap like that, we can build up a more or less complete picture of the *Wehrmacht's* dispositions in the East. Excellent, excellent,' he beamed at a proud, happy Vasili. 'But remember Vasili, be on your guard all the time. If he writes to you, let it be on a postcard. No-one distrusts a man who receives his mail in the form of cards. When you meet him at a *treff*, make it in a well-frequented place like a swimming-pool or a store, and ensure that whatever information he passes you is camouflaged in a matchbox or a newspaper. Preferably you should met him on a Sunday or a public holiday when there are not so many flics about. Clear?'

'Clear, Trepper.'

'Indeed, the best means of contacting your Frenchman,' Trepper continued, 'is to arrange with him a certain public phone-booth. There you can use the directory to fix a *treff*.'

'How?'

'You agree with him to open a pre-determined page and there he finds the fourth word down on that page is underlined in blue pencil. That means – meeting at sixteen hundred hours. A circle in green pencil around a word on the sixth line means on the sixth day of the week, that is, the following Sunday. You see the advantage of the method?'

'Yes. Preliminary contact between the two agents is unnecessary.'

'And at the same time, in your case, you can always check that your little Frenchman comes to the telephone box unshadowed and unescorted, because you'll be watching the box unobserved when he comes to find out the time of the new *treff*.'

Vasili nodded his understanding and looked at Trepper with

* Railway Transport Office.

unconcealed admiration. 'You know your business, Trepper,' he breathed.

'I should do, Vasili, I've been in the business long enough. Anything else?'

'Just one thing.'

'Go on.' Trepper was growing impatient now. Soon the cycle-taxi would be calling for him, and he wanted to be on his way; he never liked to make any *treff* longer than an hour. It was an elementary security precaution.

'Margarete has heard something about a certain photograph which has been circulated to each German H.Q. and office.'

'So?'

'Well, it seems the Boche are looking for the man and think him important enough to have his photo on display in every one of their offices.'

'What's so new about that?' Trepper said, picking up his expensive black-leather briefcase, and homburg. 'They often do things like that.'

Vasili hesitated, his forehead creased in a worried frown. 'Well, naturally I haven't seen the photo – it has been limited to chiefs and senior clerks. But as far as I can make out from her description – and you know what women are when it comes to describing anything exactly – ' 'Yes? Get on with it, Vasili,' Trepper interrupted hurriedly. Down below he could hear the crunch of the cycle-taxi's wheels over the gravel path.

'Well, it seems that the description of the wanted man,' Vasili bit his bottom lip,' could just fit you . . .'

Sitting in the back of the cycle-taxi as it sped down the hill to the little station, Trepper was so engrossed in Vasili's strange revelation, that he did not see the tall blond man who emerged from the trees after the taxi had hissed by, and who now began to plod back the way he had come.

The message on the 15,600 kilocycle range came in promptly at the expected time. Swiftly he slipped on his earphones and began to note the six-letter blocks. It was very short and the transmission stopped after not more than two minutes.

Hastily he took out his code book and began the deciphering. It was the info he needed. He guessed it had come from an SOE* source or perhaps by courtesy of De Gaulle's

* Special Operations Executive, a British Intelligence organisation.

London-based intelligence service. Anyway, it didn't matter where it had come from. The important thing was he had it; now he would be able to carry the op. a step further.

He glanced down at the decode again, and memorized it. '*Abwehr H.Q. dealing with Orchestra located old Sûrete H.Q., Rue de Sausaies.*' He slipped the rice paper into his mouth, chewed it to pulp and swallowed it.

He was ready for the next plant...

CHAPTER FIVE

Fat Heinz entered the office without knocking.

Sprawled full length on the office chaise-longue, drunk, but with his emaciated ashen face still drawn with pain, Stahl looked up, startled. Peipe dropped his pen and snapped, 'Have you forgotten all military courtesy, you barrel of lard? My God, man, are you looking forward to a quick posting to the Eastern Front?'

'Excuse me, gentlemen, excuse me, gentlemen!' Sergeant Heinz gasped, his fat red face gleaming with excitement. 'But this just came in. I was carried away. I didn't think that . . .' He broke off the breathless flood of words and handed the cheap scrap of paper to a puzzled, angry Captain Peipe.

Wordlessly the latter snatched it, without even a 'thank-you', a sign of just how bad his nerves were after so many months of unsuccessfully hunting for the new Orchestra.

It was printed in block letters, in pencil, and written in French, some of it appallingly badly spelled. But after his eyes had flown along the first line, his attention was no longer held by the terrible orthography, but by the message's contents.

Peipe read it through once more with growing excitement, while Fat Heinz, equally excited, waited for his reaction.

It came. 'My God, you fat rogue!' Peipe exploded, feeling happier than he had for weeks. 'If there's anything in this, there'll be a three-day pass for you to go and see that whore you're keeping in Brussels!'

Fat Heinz beamed.

Stahl looked up slowly, with a groan of pain. 'What's all the racket about?' he asked.

Peipe didn't answer his question immediately. Instead, he asked one of his own. 'Where did it come from, Heinz?'

'The frog gendarme on duty at the door – in the concierge's cage – found it this morning when he came back from having a piss – excuse me, sir – passing water in that filthy bog of theirs out back. You can tell what their security is—'

'For God's sake,' Stahl interrupted, sitting up, face resting on one hand as if he were too weary to raise himself any further, 'what the devil are the two of you chattering about like a pair of old washerwomen, eh?'

'This,' Peipe answered, and handed him the scrap of paper.

Stahl pulled out the nickel-rimmed spectacles that he was forced to wear since the terrible, wasting disease had started to enter its final stages and stared down at the words, looking, for all the world, like some ancient petty clerk at the end of his miserable career.

Hoarsely he read them aloud, translating slowly as he read: '*Gentlemen of the Abwehr. There is a little rat called Henri Dupont working on the first floor of the Jeip-Fahrer Department. The rotten skirt-chasing con . . .*' Stahl looked up over the top of his glasses and asked, '*Con?*'

'Cunt, Herr Stahl,' Fat Heinz supplied the translation obligingly.

'Thank you, Heinz,' Stahl said and read on: '*could tell you something important about what you gentlemen seek, if the right methods were applied. And I hope that you know what methods I mean – and I hope too, the bastard fries in hell.*' Signed simply '*A Friend*'. Stahl took off his glasses slowly and looked at an expectant Peipe. 'A denunciation, eh?'

'It looks like it. You know we get a lot of them. People hoping that we Boche will pay off their private scores for them. But this is different.'

'How do you mean?'

'Well, as you know, this is not the main *Abwehr* H.Q. in Paris. We are strictly a sub-unit searching for the Orchestra. Besides, he seems to know that we are looking for one special object.' Without waiting for Stahl's reaction, he swung round on Sergeant Heinz. 'What is this *Jein-Fahrer* Department business Heinz? It's a new one on me.'

'Jeip is an abbreviation, sir.'

'And?'

'It stands for '*Jeder einmal in Paris*'.* It's a leave organisation. Those Front swine have their names pulled out of a hat by their battalion C.O. If they strike lucky, *Jeip* arranges for

* 'Everybody in Paris one time.'

them to be transported to Paris so that they can dip their wicks. Excuse me, sir,' Fat Heinz smiled wickedly, 'I meant, see the cultural treasures of the French capital.'

'Do you mean that those folks in the *Jeip* Department know where every unit on the Eastern Front is stationed, Heinz?'

'I would imagine so, sir. They have to arrange the transport and billets for the Front swine.'

Peipe looked at Stahl, who had sat up, his face grey with pain, but new fire in his faded eyes. 'Don't you see?' he rapped.

'I certainly do. The bastard could pass on our whole order of battle in the East.' Stahl grabbed his hat. 'Come on, what are you waiting for, Peipe?'

Their boots echoed hollowly down the long dark corridor of the cellars in Fresnes Prison. There was a smell of burning and a stench of mould. Peipe's stomach churned. He knew what that signified. Even before the French guard opened the door into the room, he knew what the place was intended for – *torture*!

'Please, gentlemen.' The Frenchman stepped to one side politely and extended his right hand, as if he were ushering them into his best room.

Stahl and Peipe passed inside.

The room was bare, its walls rough and dripping with moisture. It's furniture was limited: a table, a three-legged stool, a newish-looking telephone attached to the far wall, and – very ominously – a thick hempen rope attached to a pulley on the ceiling. Peipe, his heart sinking, didn't need to be told that the dark stains on the rope were from blood, human blood.

'One moment, gentlemen,' the French warder said. 'The prisoner will be here in an instant.'

Stahl slumped on the table and took out his flask. He offered it to Peipe, and for once the *Abwehr* Captain accepted it. He needed a drink to face what was to come.

A minute later there came the sound of footsteps ringing hollowly down the long stone corridor: one pair firm, confident, metallic! the other, slow, hesitant, weak.

The torturer came into the cell first. He was an enormous, shaven-headed sergeant in the *Gendarmerie*, with a blaze of First World War battle ribbons on his broad blue chest. He flung the two officers a tremendous salute and said in harsh

Alsatian German, 'Sergeant Jean-Paul Heidemann at your service, gentlemen.'

Peipe recognised the accent. The torturer was a native of that eastern province, where both French and German were spoken.

'All right,' Stahl croaked. 'Bring him in.'

'In, you Communist shit!' the sergeant said in French.

An ashen-faced little man, whose right cheek was already badly bruised, entered, holding to his trousers, for the French had removed his belt and shoelaces to prevent him from committing suicide. It was standard operating procedure at Fresnes.

Peipe took out the photograph they had found on the ID card in Brussels. 'Do you know this man?' he asked. 'Was this the man you worked for?'

The little prisoner shook his head.

The sergeant gave him a brutal dig in the ribs, so that he gasped with pain, and snarled: 'Answer when the German officer speaks to you.'

'No, I don't know him.'

The sergeant hit him again. 'Put a "sir" on that,' he commanded.

'No, sir.'

Peipe sighed wearily. 'All right,' he said to the sergeant, 'take over. You know what we want to know, Sergeant.'

The sergeant beamed, as if he were going to enjoy what happened next. 'Yes, sir,' he said heartily, and rolled up his sleeves with dramatic, anticipatory slowness to reveal massive arms, covered with black hairs. 'All right, *sale con*, I'm going to ask you some questions and I want answers – and I'd better tell you now that Jean-Paul Heidemann has been known in the past to get a confession out of an Egyptian mummy.' He laughed uproariously at his own joke, while Stahl stared moodily at the ashen-faced prisoner and Peipe bit his lip anxiously.

'Now, what's the name of the bastard you worked for?'

The prisoner said nothing.

The sergeant grinned pleasurably. 'All right, you little shit, if that's the way you want to play it, we'll have you do a few tricks.'

The next half hour was the worst Peipe had ever spent. The sergeant made the little man drop his slacks and bend over the stool. The prisoner screamed shrilly at what the sadistic Alsatian did to him, but still he did not answer the question.

'You probably liked that, eh?' the sergeant said cheerfully. 'Let's see if you like this.'

He slipped a pair of handcuffs on the man's wrists, and attaching the rope to it, hoisted him up so that only his toes touched the floor. For what seemed a long time, the sergeant puffed at a cigarette, while the prisoner, his teeth clenched tightly together, the sweat streaming down his pain-contorted face, tried to support his weight on his toes.

'All right, shit, who was your employer?'

The prisoner shook his head, obviously not trusting himself to speak.

The sergeant stubbed out his cigarette on the back of the prisoner's skinny neck. The Frenchman screamed. The sergeant gave a pleasurable gasp. 'So you still want to play games, my little friend? You want to play more tricks, eh?'

He untied the rope. With a sigh of relief the little prisoner sank to the floor, his eyes closed. The sergeant ignored him. Opening the drawer of the little table he took out a small piece of piano wire and a stick. Turning, he beamed at the two officers. 'The tourniquet. It gets a bit noisy but they always talk in the end with the tourniquet.'

Stahl nodded, but said nothing. Peipe looked at the frail body of the man crumpled on the floor and prayed he would talk.

Swiftly and expertly, the sergeant tied the man's ankles together with the piano wire and inserted the stick inside the wire. He kicked the prisoner savagely in the ribs. 'Open your peepers,' he commanded.

The prisoner did so, and stared up at his torturer with undisguised fear.

'Now, I'm asking you again. Who was your employer?' His voice lost its gruff tone for a moment. 'Now lad, be reasonable. You're going to have to sing in the end. Why not spare yourself a lot of agony. Talk now.'

Doggedly the prisoner shook his head.

'All right, have it your way. Here we go, you Red turd.' With a grunt, he turned the stick, once, twice. The wire cut deep into the man's ankles. The prisoner's body arched like a bow and he screamed, his mouth wide-open and taut with pain. Gasping joyfully, now solely concerned with the pleasure the torture gave him, the sergeant turned again – and again. Blood, thick and red, started to stream through the man's socks and over the wire which had almost vanished into his flesh. He writhed and struggled, strangled, inhuman cries coming from his throat, while Peipe stared down at him, eyes full of horror. He opened his mouth. He couldn't stand it any longer.

Surprisingly enough, Stahl beat him to it. 'All right, Sergeant, you've had your fun!' he croaked. 'Stop it. He'll sing now.'

Reluctantly the sergeant did as he was commanded. He released the stick. The prisoner sank back on the floor, sobbing with relief.

'I'll talk . . . I'll talk,' he gasped. 'But not – *that*.'

The sergeant, his face crimson with the effort and covered by a greasy film of sweat, looked at the two silent officers proudly. 'Didn't I tell you, gentlemen?' he boasted. 'Brave or cowardly, they always sing in the finish.' He poked his stick in the man's skinny ribs. 'All right, ape-shit, sit up and talk.'

Stahl took out his flask and handed it to the prisoner. 'Drink,' he said.

The prisoner took a sip of the cognac and coughed as the fiery spirit coursed through his pain-racked body, while the sergeant looked on contemptuously at such weakness on the part of the German.

'Well?' Peipe demanded.

'I can't tell you much.'

'Let us be the judge of that. How did you meet the man you gave the information to, and what was his name?'

The prisoner licked his cracked, blood-stained lips, but he was obviously beaten; he had no resisitance left. 'In the Hotel Majestic,' he began. Peipe looked at Stahl significantly. 'I had to go there about a billeting problem for an officer from the front and they made me wait at the reception. We got talking there—'

'Go on,' Peipe urged, when the man appeared to be about to stop.

'Well, at first I thought he was a German, because he spoke French with a foreign accent – he was in civilian clothes of course. But after we'd met a couple of times in bars and cafes, I knew he wasn't.'

'What nationality was he?' Peipe asked.

'I don't know. All I know was that he wasn't French and he wasn't German.'

'All right, get on with it.'

'Well, after a while he asked me if I were a patriot. I said I was, although I worked for the Bo – the German authorities. One has to eat, even in wartime.' He made a pathetic attempt to throw out his skinny chest, and failed badly. 'Then it was that he asked me to supply him with information about the men on leave from the Front.'

'All right, you little French fighting-cock,' Stahl said in German, 'don't tell me you didn't know his name.'

Peipe translated, and the Frenchman answered. 'He told me to call him Jo-Jo, and that's the only name I had for him.'

'And didn't he tell you what service he worked for?' Peipe said hastily, trying to save the man from further torture.

'Yes, he said he worked for the British.'

'Smart bastard,' Stahl grunted.

'And how did you contact him?' Peipe continued.

'Well, he has something wrong with his legs. He is small like me, but his legs are swollen like an elephant's and he doesn't like walking far, so we'd contact each other through the phone-box just outside the *Jeip* office.' Swiftly the prisoner explained how Jo-Jo arranged to contact him through the markings in the Paris telephone directory in the phone-box and how they would meet in the Luxembourg Gardens which were close by, so that Jo-Jo didn't have too far to walk.

'So you went to the phone booth every day to check if there was a message for you?' Peipe asked.

The prisoner said nothing, but Peipe knew from the look of self-disgust in his eyes that he was right. Swiftly he turned and translated for Stahl's sake, while the prisoner hung his head, obviously realising that he had delivered Jo-Jo into the hands of his enemies.

Stahl sat bolt upright when Peipe had finished his translation. He grabbed his hat and rose to his feet. 'All right, Captain,' he cried with new energy, 'what are we waiting for? Let's go.'

'To where?'

'To stake out that telephone booth. We have an appointment with Monsieur Jo-Jo!'

But after twenty-four hours of close surveillance of the telephone booth outside the *Jeip* H.Q., Stahl was forced to concede that Jo-Jo was not going to turn up. The unknown spy had obviously been alerted – somehow or other – by the fact that the little French clerk had not paid his daily visit to the phone-box to check whether a *treff* had been arranged.

As he said to a disappointed Peipe, after Fat Heinz had

reported that no-one suspicious had approached the booth, 'I think this Jo-Jo must have got wise to us, Captain.'

'Yes, you must be right,' Peipe admitted, glumly. 'Now we're back to square one.'

Stahl shook his head. 'Not exactly, my dear Captain. We have a lead, you know.'

'Not much of one.'

'Well, we know that here we have a civilian who apparently is not German or French, yet has the right to go in and out of the Hotel Majestic – and you know what a fuss they make there about security. It's probably easier to get into heaven than that dump.'

'Agreed, but there must be several non-Germans from the varied Allied liaison teams – the Bulgarians and the Rumanians and the like – who have permission to enter the Majestic.'

Stahl nodded his agreement. 'Admittedly, admittedly. But you are forgetting one thing, Peipe.'

'And that is?'

'That little Frenchman's description of this Jo-Jo.'

'I can't say there was much description. 'Peipe shrugged.' He said Jo-Jo looked pretty much like himself, small and skinny.'

'With one exception, Peipe. His legs.' Stahl smiled at the other man. 'Legs like an elephant, our Frenchman said. That should be a give-away. *Legs like an elephant*...'

FIVE: THE CONDUCTOR IS ARRESTED

At dawn on November 19th, 1942, a thick fog descended upon the ruined city of Stalingrad, where General Paulus's Sixth German Army was trying to dislodge the Russian defenders from the ruins.

It came just as the Russian weathermen had predicted it would, and the undersized yellow-faced troops of the Siberian rifle divisions were not slow in taking advantage of it. Without the normal artillery bombardment, the little fur-clad men started to slip into the German positions. The Germans rallied. But they had been caught off guard; and the Russians were coming in battalions, brigades, divisions, corps, whole armies. They seemed to be everywhere in the ruins, and nothing could stop them. By midday they had made a clean breakthrough and were streaming through the rear of the German defences, chasing the German's ragged, fearful Italian and Rumanian allies before them. By late afternoon they had made a deep penetration; and by nightfall, when the darkness descended once more and the fighting started to peter out for that day, they were thirty miles to Paulus's rear. The trap, which would finish off Paulus's 400,000-strong army, had been well and truly sprung.

Now the Red Army would commence its long march westwards, and the victory to which the Red Orchestra had contributed so much, was inevitable . . .

The German bombers had been again. Here and there over the jagged skyline of the capital, slow pillars of oily black smoke ascended into the morning sky. Yet Parliament Square remained oddly serene, and the men crossing the square, some in uniform, some in the black dress of senior officials, were as immaculate and as contained as if this were just another routine November day. One by one they strode by the brooding, soot-marked statues of Lincoln and Lord Beaconsfield, and entered Number 2, Great George Street.

At the sandbagged guard-post at the entrance they were confronted with the war again. Hard-eyed sentries of the Coldstream Guards, everyone of them over six foot, scrutinized their passes very carefully, even those of the soldiers who wore the red gorgets and golden lions of the Imperial General Staff. One by one they filed into the neon-lit, antiseptic atmosphere of the command post, passing through the corridors shored up by ancient timbers taken from Admiral Nelson's men-o'-war, past the map room, of solid concrete, reinforced by old London tramrails, and into the underground conference room.

Their voices, usually so confident and self-assured, became subdued in the little room, which in the autumn of 1942 was the heart of the whole British Empire. It was not a very spacious place and nothing about its furniture revealed that from here every important decision, affecting the lives and destinies of the many millions who made up the world's greatest empire, was made: a cheap portrait of George VI, a lithograph of London Bridge, leather chairs, a solid, wooden-framed clock, inscribed with the words, 'Victoria R.I., Ministry of Works, 1889'. Nothing much; even the whirring fan in the ceiling was of an ancient, asthmatic vintage. Indeed, the only clue to the real purpose of this small underground chamber was the small figurine in the centre of the well-polished old conference table – that of a dancing faun, suggestive of dark, evil spirits at work in remote, tangled forests.

The Prime Minister entered almost immediately after the last conference member had taken his place. He was dressed in his usual jump-suit, a one-piece combination with a zip-fastener at the front, so that with his fat, round, red, unwrinkled face, he looked like some overgrown, bald-headed baby. Since the recent victory in the Western Desert he had been in a high good mood and this morning was no exception. Waving a large Havana at them happily, he told them to sit down, taking the chair at the head of the table himself.

He dipped the end of his big cigar in the glass of brandy already poured and waiting for him at his right elbow, sucked it pleasurably and then lit the Havana with a flourish. 'Right, gentlemen,' he said through a cloud of blue smoke, which almost obscured his broad cheerful face. 'What have you for me, this grey November morning?'

Field-Marshall Alan Brooke, the sour, bespectacled Chief of the Imperial General Staff, answered. 'Prime Minister, before we go on to details of *Torch*,* I'd like you to listen to General Menzies.'

Churchill looked to the far end of the table. The three of them were there – 'the terrible triplets', he called them to Brooke behind their backs: Menzies, the Chief, pale, reticent and frail-looking; Dansey, his deputy, squat, red-faced and pushy, looking like a commercial traveller on the make;

* Code name for the landings in N. Africa.

and Vivian, too upper-class to be true, all apologies and hesitancy.

'Ah, the gentlemen of the Old Firm,' Churchill exclaimed good-humouredly. 'And what have the cloak-and-dagger merchants to offer in the way of skulduggery, eh?'

Vivian's long refined face looked pained. Churchill pointed to the plaque behind him on the wall and recited the words on it from memory: '"We are bred up to feel it a disgrace to succeed by falsehood . . . we will keep hammering along with the conviction that honesty is the best policy, and that truth always wins in the long run. These pretty little sentiments do well for a child's copy-book, but a man who acts on them had better sheathe his sword for ever."' He paused, and gave a red-faced, embarrassed Vivian the full benefit of his toothless smile – he had forgotten to wear his false teeth yet again – before saying, 'So, my dear Colonel Vivian, do not feel embarrassed. After all, Field-Marshal Wolseley, the epitome of Victorian morality, wrote those words over eighty years ago.'

'Sorry, sir,' Vivian mumbled, more embarrassed than ever.

Churchill turned his attention to Menzies, Vivian's Chief. 'Well, General?' he demanded.

'It's Operation Cuckoo Egg, Prime Minister,' said the pale-faced Head of the Secret Intelligence Service.

Churchill sniffed with distaste. 'What a terrible cover-name, Menzies. No dignity about it.' He waved his cigar at the other man. 'Yes, I recollect the operation. Please carry on. What have you found out since we last discussed the operation?'

'A great deal, Prime Minister. Colonel Dansey?' He turned to his second-in-command.

Dansey, always eager to ensure that Churchill was aware of his existence, for he wanted a 'K'* before the war was over (it would be good for business), began to read his brief hurriedly: 'Their organisation was developed in '39–'40 to work against this country. In mid-'40, it started to turn its attention to Germany. One year later it was spread over most of Western Europe, including the Reich itself. At the end of that year it suffered a severe blow when most of its Berlin off-shoot was rounded up. However, the head of the organisation, obviously from all reports a very able man indeed—'

* i.e. a knighthood.

'For a Bolshie,' Churchill broke in again, brandy glass in hand.

'For a Bolshie, sir,' Dansey agreed cheerfully, happy that the great man had joked with him. 'Well, this resourceful spymaster has now put his organisation, especially in France, on a very sound footing. Indeed, if the organisation there run by the gentlemen of the Ministry of Economic Warfare were so sound, we of the – er – Old Firm would be much happier with our French situation.' He looked pointedly at Minister Dalton, the head of the rival Intelligence agency, the SOE.

The tall grey-haired minister, who affected a wing collar, flushed. 'Prime Minister,' he began, 'I must protest—'

Churchill waved him to be silent, happy that Dansey had managed to take a rise out of the self-opinionated Socialist, whom he knew would be after his own job one of these days. 'Not so touchy, Dalton,' he said. 'Remember the Old Firm is *the* senior service, and like the Royal Navy they guard their special position jealously.'

Dalton muttered something, but dropped the subject. Churchill nodded to a self-satisfied Dansey.

Dansey continued to read his brief, while Menzies stared at the table with his hooded pale eyes, as if he could see something there, known only to him. Swiftly and expertly, Dansey briefed the Prime Minister on the ramifications of the espionage ring in Europe. 'In short, Prime Minister,' he summed up, 'they have established a very effective spy organization, which so far has been proof against any attempt on the part of the Hun to break it.'

Churchill smiled faintly to himself. A man like Dansey would say 'Hun'.

'Thank you, Colonel,' he said, and looked at Menzies. 'And the problem, General?'

Menzies took his eyes off the table. He looked at Churchill's happy red face as if he were seeing it for the first time, and for a moment the PM felt a shudder of fear; the head of the Intelligence service had more power than he had himself. He wondered what it must be like to be able to command blackmail, bribery, sexual perversion, even murder, without having to account to anyone. He told himself that no one should have that much power.

'The problem?' Menzies echoed the word in that curiously toneless voice of his. 'It is this, sir. Every indication is that the Boche will no longer be able to stop the Red Army in its march westwards.'

Churchill nodded his agreement, his face suddenly grim. 'They broke through at Stalingrad this morning – in depth. We heard it from Ultra this morning.* If Hitler persists on trying to hold the Front there, which I think he will, he'll lose his 6th Army and then it will be Napoleon's retreat all over again.'

Politely, his pale frail face completely without expression, Menzies waited till Churchill had finished. Then he continued as if the PM had not even spoken. 'Once the Russians arrive in Central Europe,' he said, 'I have every reason to believe that the Red Orchestra, as the Gestapo call this spy ring, will return to its original function – it will commence spying on our own forces. The *raison d'être* for Operation Cuckoo Egg was to find out the details of the spy ring and pinpoint its head. We have done both. Now there is the question of a decision. 'Menzies' pale eyes gleamed for a moment and they held Churchill's curious gaze for a moment before dropping them to the table once more. 'A decision which only you can make, sir.'

'And it is?'

'The Russians are our allies, but they may well become our enemies again, as they were before the war.'

Churchill nodded his agreement.

'So the decision has to be made. Do we let this spy ring continue to function and help the Red Army to its victories, in the knowledge that one day it might well be turned against the interests of the British Empire? Or should we destroy it now, while we are still in a position to do so?'

Brooke, the Chief of Staff, as much a Communist-hater as the rest of them in that little underground room, looked shocked at such duplicity. He was the only one there to do so. Civilians and military alike, they had walked the corridors of power at Whitehall long enough to know that this was how one survived at the top.

Churchill took another sip of his brandy. 'I once wrote that battles are won by slaughter and manoeuvre. The greater the general, the more he contributes in manoeuvre, the less he demands in slaughter. Well, my dear gentlemen of the

* Ultra, the British top-secret radio operation, with which the British could read all messages sent by the German High Command via the Enigma coding machine.

Old Firm, what manoeuvre do you suggest to avoid the slaughter that may well come?'

Surprisingly enough, it was the usually tongue-tied Colonel Vivian who made the final suggestion. 'I recommend we betray this man Trepper to the Germans . . .'

CHAPTER ONE

Stahl and Peipe arrested Vasili Maximov two days after they started their observation of the entrance of the Hotel Majestic. The skinny man came waddling in, with one of the plainest women it had been Peipe's misfortune to see clutching his arm fearfully, as if he might tear himself away from her at any moment, overcome by her ugliness. But Stahl leaning against the receptionist's desk, cheap cigar in his mouth, did not see the woman. His eyes were fixed on the skinny little civilian's legs, as he waddled towards the lift, with obvious difficulty.

'Like an elephant's, the Frog said,' he reminded Peipe.

'Yes, a civilian who is neither German nor French, with swollen legs,' the other man whispered. He turned and spoke to the corporal who ran the reception. 'Who is that man?' he asked.

'Oh, that's the Baron,' answered the sleek-haired corporal, who had once worked at the Adlon Hotel in Berlin before the war and knew his clients well, as anyone who had been trained in that famous hotel should. 'Baron Vasili Maximov, engaged to be married to Fraulein Margarete Hoffman-Scholz, the lady.'

'A Russian?' Peipe snapped.

'*White* Russian,' the corporal corrected him with the hotelier's attention to minor detail. 'An emigré.'

Peipe was no longer listening. He grabbed Stahl's arm 'Come on,' he said urgently. 'That's him all right.'

Five minutes later, the little Russian was singing heartily, while the plain secretary sobbed, heart-broken, on the rumpled bed.

'Don't hit me . . . you don't need to . . . I'll tell you everything,' he had said immediately.

And he did. He told them about the *Jiep* clerk and his other espionage contacts, the words pouring from his lips, while the woman sobbed and sobbed.

Stahl took out the picture. 'Is this your boss?' he asked.

Vasili nodded, 'Yes, that's him – Trepper.'

Stahl looked at Peipe in barely concealed triumph. 'So that's his name. Trepper, eh?'

'Yes.'

'Is he a Russian?' Peipe asked.

'I think so, but you can never tell these days. Since the Revolution the language has changed . . .'

'How do you contact him?' Stahl cut him short brutally. 'Do you know where this Trepper lives?'

'No, I don't know where he lives.' Vasili hesitated for an instant. Stahl hit him across the face. It was a routine, light blow, meant simply to hurry him up. But a suddenly ashen-faced Vasili took the blow as a forerunner of the terrible tortures probably to come.

'Don't . . . please don't hit me,' he cried fearfully. 'I'll tell you. I contact him through my sister.' He told them about Anna in a frightened spate of words.

'And when do you see him?' Peipe asked.

'About once a month. Anna – my sister – she contacts him for me.'

Peipe turned to Fat Heinz standing at the door, drawn pistol in his pudgy fist. 'All right, Heinz, take him away,' he commanded.

At the words, the plain woman, her raddled face made uglier still by the tears, sprang from the bed and tried to hold her lover back. But Heinz tugged fiercely and she gave way. '*Vasili, Vasili!*' she cried piteously, falling to his feet.

'Well, at least I won't have to sleep with her again,' the little Baron said with an attempt at his old humour, and then without another word, he allowed himself to be taken away to an unknown fate.

Instinctively Anna knew who they were as the long black Citroen swung through the gate and into the gravel drive, nudging its way through the excited crowd of laughing, screaming, yelling patients who were staring up at the tree where the naked exhibitionist was giving one of his usual performances to the horror of the 'grey mouse', who was trying to coax him down. Anna acted automatically. Flinging open the window of her study, she screamed urgently: 'Stop them! They're coming to take you away for being naughty – to put you behind bars, where there'll be no more trees!'

'*To take me away!*' the naked exhibitionist yelled, and dropped straight out of the tree onto the Citroen's bonnet. The driver braked instinctively and the next moment all was chaos, with the frantic lunatics, scared that they were going to be taken away, hammering at the car doors and rocking it back and forth alarmingly in an attempt to overturn it.

Inside, Peipe and Stahl clung furiously to the straps to avoid being thrown to the floor, staring at the crazed, frightened faces peering in at them, while the shock-haired exhibitionist, his sexual predilections forgotten for once, directed the operation.

'God Almighty,' Stahl croaked, 'where the devil have we landed now?'

'I'll tell you,' Peipe gasped. struggling to free his pistol, while he was thrown to one side. 'In the nut mill. This is a lunatic asylum!'

In that instant, he managed at last to draw his pistol. He didn't hesitate. Rolling down the window with his one hand, he picked up the pistol again and fired a quick burst into the grey November sky.

The shot had the effect he desired. Screaming with alarm and fear, the lunatics scattered for cover, bowling each other over and clawing at one another in their haste to escape. Peipe flung open the door and spotted the 'grey mouse' sprawled full-length on the grass, her grey skirt thrown up to reveal knee-length flannel knickers.

'Hey you, sister,' he called.

The 'grey mouse' sat up and hastily smoothed down her skirt, her plain, honest face crimson with embarrassment. 'Sir?'

'Where do I find the owner?' he called urgently. 'Doctor Anna Maximov. Hurry please. Every moment is precious.'

The 'grey mouse' pointed to the leaded window on the second floor. 'Up there, sir.'

Peipe flung a glance in that direction and caught a glimpse of a fat face and a plump beringed hand holding what appeared to be a phone.

'Come on, Stahl!' he snapped swiftly. 'She's on to us. At the double!'

With the Gestapo man gasping frighteningly at his heels, Peipe ran for the house, pistol still in his hand.

But it was already too late. By the time he and Fat Heinz had broken through the door to face the apparently completely calm fat blonde woman who stood at the far end of the big desk, waiting for them, he knew that she already had warned their quarry.

'All right, no playing about,' he snapped, angry at being cheated yet again. 'What number did you call?'

'I shall tell you one thing. After that I shall say no more,' the woman announced, her voice completely under control. 'You may beat me as much as you wish – and you probably will – but you won't get anything out of me, unlike that little gutless brother of mine. Now I shall speak no more.'

Fat Heinz doubled his fist. 'I don't like to hit a lady, but I think I could hit this fat cheeky bitch without too much trouble.'

Peipe shook his head. Instead he picked up the phone which she had obviously used to warn the mystery man, Trepper, and snapped, 'M'selle, I want to know the telephone number of the person last called on this phone. Our number is . . .'

In the corner, the fat woman clenched her fists in impotent fury.

'The birds have flown,' Stahl croaked as they strode through the wide-open door of the little brothel.

Peipe agreed glumly. The hall, which smelled of sweat and ancient vice, was obviously empty.

Together, followed by a wide-eyed Heinz, they walked down the long hall, decorated with faded yellow photographs of women, in the cropped haircuts of the 1920s, displaying their beefy charms or indulging in intricate, impossible couplings with animals and other women.

They flung open the door of the first cubby-hole. The room, its sole decoration a bed and a bidet, was empty, but it was obvious that whoever had lived there had fled hastily. There was a pair of unwashed silken knickers hanging from the bidet and cheap, sickly-smelling face powder had been spilled on the floor.

'She's going to catch a nasty cold without these,' Stahl said, holding up the knickers.

Peipe grunted and moved on to the next room. It, too, was empty, Anna's telephone call had had its effect.

'You can bet your last mark that the fellow who owned this knocking-shop warned friend Trepper, too,' Stahl said, as they entered the heavily furnished lounge, the place where the male visitors to the cheap brothel selected their 'little rabbits' for the night.

'You can say that again,' Peipe answered gloomily. He raised his voice. 'Have you found the phone yet, Heinz? We might be able to get some prints off it that could be useful. The Sûrete will surely have—' He stopped suddenly. Fat Heinz was staring down curiously at the long-stemmed ivory-handled phone on the little table in the corner.

'What's the matter with you – the cat got your tongue?' Peipe demanded.

'No, sir,' Heinz answered hastily. 'But what do you make of this? It was propped carefully against the phone.'

'Of what?'

'This.' The fat sergeant turned round, his plump face bewildered, and handed Peipe what was obviously a visiting card.

Peipe held it to the light – the room was very dark – and read aloud what was written on the card in copper-plate writing:

'Dr Malepate, Family Dentist,
13 Rue de Rivoli.
Approved by all insurance schemes.'

'Listen carefully.' Trepper's voice was hurried and flustered.

The pianist grinned at his own image in the mirror in the way lonely men do, and lit yet another cigarette from the stub of the one still burning in the overflowing ashtray. 'I'm listening,' he said calmly, telling himself the conductor had the wind up at last.

'They've hit us a bad blow. The Maximovs are under arrest – and a couple of others too.'

The pianist affected surprise and winked at himself in the fly-blown mirror.

'But we're coping. There is no need for panic. All we've got to do is to lie low until further notice. Simply suspend operations for a couple of months until the storm has blown over.'

To the pianist it seemed as if the conductor was saying the words to comfort himself.

'I understand,' he said dutifully, and took a nervous drag at his cigarette. 'But what about you? The Maximovs know you, and once the Gestapo get working on them, even Fat Anna will be singing like a little dicky-bird.'

'I know,' the conductor answered unhappily. 'I'm going to do a dive for a while. Friends of mine will be preparing a funeral for me in the next forty-eight hours. All the Gestapo will find when they come looking for me is a newly-erected gravestone with "rest in peace" on it.'

'Very smart, very smart, indeed,' the pianist said in admiration. 'That'll put the bloodhounds off for a little while, at least.'

'I hope so.'

'And then?'

'My friends will lay a false trail for the Gestapo, once they've got round to digging up the grave and finding the coffin empty. In the meantime, I'll be nice and snug in the mountains. All I need is a clean bill of health before I go into the wilderness.'

The pianist refrained from asking which mountains. That would be displaying too much curiosity; it would arouse the conductor's suspicions. Besides, if things went well, the conductor would never reach the mountains. Instead, he said, 'Don't forget your choppers. It can be hell to have toothache when you've gone underground. I know. It happened to me when I took a dive in '41.'

'I won't,' the conductor said. 'All right. That is all for the time being. Good-bye and good luck. You'll be hearing from me.'

The phone went dead.

For what seemed a long time, the pianist held the receiver, staring blankly at his own handsome pale face in the mirror, listening to the phone's never-ending *beep-beep*. Then carefully he placed it back on the cradle and lit yet another cigarette, telling himself that the operation was as good as over . . .

CHAPTER TWO

Dr Malepate was a bluff, no-nonsense man with the dentist's unfeeling eyes. But the business-like, confident expression crumpled like an eggshell when Stahl showed him his Gestapo 'dog licence'.

'But, gentlemen,' he protested, 'what have I done? I am innocent! I have nothing to do with those villains of the Resistance.' Wildly, as if he were fighting for his very life, he pointed to the cheaply coloured portrait of Marshal Pétain, the ruler of Vichy France, on the wall of his dingy surgery. 'The Marshal is my hero and—'

Impatiently, Peipe held up his hand to stop the frightened

flow of words. 'Doctor Malepate, we are not interested in your politics or yourself. We are here to enquire about one of your patients.'

Malepate breathed out an audible sigh of relief. 'Please . . . please take a seat, gentlemen,' he said in a strangled voice.

'Do you know a patient called Trepper?'

Malepate shook his head.

'Do you have any records of your patiens?' Peipe continued.

The dentist shrugged eloquently. 'Most of my patients are poor, gentlemen. What do they come for – an extraction? An injection to soothe the pain? A few tablets; No, one doesn't keep records on such people. They never come again anyway.'

'Do you know this man?' Stahl asked impatiently in his poor French, thrusting the photo under the dentist's nose.

Malepate's eyes brightened. 'Oh, yes, him I know,' he said. 'Monsieur Gilbert. A very respectable businessman from Belgium. A traveller, I believe, and a very good payer, I can assure you.'

Peipe nodded. 'And how often does this Monsieur Gilbert come for treatment?' he asked.

'He came to me first for an impacted wisdom. Since then he comes for check-ups when he is in Paris. He says that we French dentists are more thorough than our colleagues in Brussels.'

'I see. Do you expect him to come again soon?'

Malepate gave that eloquent shrug of his, full of that typical French petty-bourgeois contempt for such foolish questions. 'It is possible,' he conceded.

Stahl crooked a finger at Peipe, and together they walked into the corner, next to the dingy cabinet of surgical instruments, so that they were out of earshot. 'Listen, Peipe,' he whispered in German, while the dentist watched them apprehensively, 'that card by the phone was a definite tip-off.'

'Agreed.'

'Now, you wouldn't think that someone on the run would bother to go to the dentist, would you?'

'Not under normal circumstances,' Peipe said. 'But if our man is going to go underground, it might be just the thing he would do. Let's say he's going to some remote hideout and has a heart condition. He goes to his local sawbones for enough tablets to tide him over. Perhaps this Trepper chap has trouble with his teeth and wants to ensure that before he dives, they're all right.'

Stahl nodded his agreement, and raising his voice, Peipe asked: 'Does this Monsieur Gilbert have bad teeth?'

'Not really, sir. But to put it,' he smiled winningly, the complete dentist again, 'in laymen's terms, the enamel of his teeth is very sensitive to sugar, sweets, cakes and the like. Unfortunately Monsieur Gilbert, like most Belgians, is given to over-indulgence in such things. As a result, if he doesn't have a regular check-up, caries and pain are there in short order.'

Swiftly Peipe translated for Stahl's benefit. Stahl absorbed the information and made his decision.

'We'll slap a twenty-four hour watch on this place, Peipe,' he said. 'But don't tell old Doctor Dick there that. Just tell him this. As soon as Monsieur Gilbert telephones or calls to make an appointment – and if he's going to take a dive, he will call soon – Doctor Dick must inform us at once. Then we'll come and arrest him.'

Peipe explained what Stahl had said, in French, concluding with the words, 'So you see, Doctor, we are going to arrest this Monsieur Gilbert of yours.'

The dentist shrugged. 'Do whatever you like,' he said. 'It is no concern of mine.'

'Oh, yes it is,' Stahl said in his poor French. 'You rat, you're not going to get out of it as easily as that. You are going to co-operate whether you like it or not.' He swung round to Peipe. 'Now tell him, please, Captain, how we are going to do it.'

When Peipe had finished his explanation, Dr Malepate's face was blanched with fear. 'But what if he has a weapon? Perhaps a pistol in his pocket—'

'Then I suggest you keep your big fingers stuck down his throat so that he can't pull it out,' Stahl sneered. 'And woe betide you, Doctor Malepate, if the bastard escapes us this time.'

With that, the two of them stalked out, leaving Dr Malepate holding on to his worn leather chair, as if he might fall to the floor if he didn't have some support.

CHAPTER THREE

Trepper's relaxed mood vanished as the doctor ushered him into the dingy waiting room its, dark walls decorated with yellowing photographs of country scenes, which were supposed to encourage the patients to forget their pains.

In the last twenty-four hours he had acted swiftly, and

everything had gone strictly according to plan. His couriers had sped to half a dozen cities, both in France and in the Low Countries, to warn his agents to go underground for the time being; the Party had already produced a doctor who would sign his death certificate; and his American mistress had already begun the long trip to the Auvergne Mountains to get the hide-out ready for him. Once this damned check was over, he would die, taking final refuge in the Beyond.

But now as he took his seat, his mood changed to one of unease, even apprehension. Normally the working-class practice was packed with shabby, pain-racked men and women. Now it was empty save for an old woman, who appeared to be asleep. He frowned. As always he had checked the place for a means of escape in case anything happened. Usually, the office door was open leading to a passage which would make an ideal escape route. Today it was closed. But before Trepper could heed the little voice, warning him to get out of Number 13 Rue de Rivoli, while the going was still good, Doctor Malepate had opened the door to the surgery and invited him to enter.

Trepper dismissed his apprehension and sat down in the chair, saying, 'Please try to make it as quick as you can, Doctor. I've got an urgent and important business appointment in one hour from now.'

'I shall do my best, Monsieur Gilbert,' Malepate said, easing the patient's head back on the leather head-piece and taking up his probe, ears on the alert for the sounds which would indicate that the Gestapo had arrived.

'Tut, tut,' he forced himself to say, as time began to drag and there was still no sign of the Boche. 'What have we here?' He scraped at Gilbert's molars.'

'What is it, Doctor?' Trepper asked thickly.

'Looks as if you've been naughty again,' Malepate said. 'You Belgians, you just can't leave those sweet things alone, even when sugar costs a small fortune on the black market.'

'Will you have to drill?'

'I'm afraid so. But it won't hurt. It's not much of a hole.'

He pulled his finger out of the patient's mouth and said routinely, 'Please rinse.' Hastily he turned, so that Gilbert could not see the look on his face, and started to busy himself with the old-fashioned treadle drill.

Trepper leaned back against the head-rest and closed his eyes, as if he were preparing himself to meet the pain to come. Malepate started suddenly. There was a sharp metallic clink outside. Instinctively he knew the sound was that of handcuffs being opened. The Gestapo had arrived. Hastily he swung round, and wadding the side of Gilbert's mouth with cotton wool, he started to work the foot treadle. He was in a cold sweat and his hand was trembling so much that he could hardly direct the drill on the healthy tooth. But he knew he must keep Gilbert down – now.

Gilbert tensed, both hands grabbing the arm rests. The drill was obviously hurting. Little chips of tooth started to fly. There was a smell of burning. He was working the drill too fast. By a sheer effort of will, Malepate forced himself to slow down. His eyes shifted to the door. It was opening cautiously. They were coming in. He breathed a hasty prayer heavenwards and tensed. If there was any shooting, he would fling himself behind the instrument cabinet. It was metal. It should keep off the bullets.

Stahl came in first. He was in his stocking feet. In one hand, he clutched a pistol; in the other, a pair of gleaming steel handcuffs. Behind him, Peipe appeared; he also held a pistol in his one hand. Even in his own panic-stricken state, Doctor Malepate could see just how nervous the two Germans were. The man he was treating must obviously be a very big fish indeed.

'Just a moment more, Monsieur Gilbert,' he forced himself to say, preparing himself for the dive behind the instrument cabinet, 'then it'll be all over.' He gulped and worked the treadle as if his very life depended upon it.

Stahl acted. With surprising speed for such an old and obviously very sick man, he knocked the dentist to one side, ripped the drill out of Trepper's mouth and stuck the pistol against his chest.

'Don't make a move, Trepper!' he cried.

Peipe, too, thrust his pistol at the man in the chair, while Stahl lowered his and slipped the cuffs around Trepper's hands. They clicked together with a comfortingly solid metallic sound.

Surprisingly enough Trepper recovered quicker than any of them. Abruptly his broad tough face lit up and he said: 'My congratulations, gentlemen. You have done a good job of work.' His voice was calm and completely under control.

Without protest, he allowed himself to be hauled to his feet. Just as he reached the door, Malepate, suddenly realising what happened to traitors in wartime France, said nervously: 'I want you to know that this is none of my doing, Monsieur Gilbert.'

'Of course not,' Trepper answered, master of the situation now. 'What do I owe you?'

Solemnly Dr Malepate said, 'Under the circumstances, Monsieur, please be my guest.'

Trepper winked at Stahl and went out, as if he didn't have a care in the world.

The signal that Vivian handed Menzies was simple. It read:

'From: Wily

To: C

Trepper arrested this afternoon. Confirmed.'

General Menzies dropped it carelessly into the 'out' tray. 'Well, that's that, Vivian,' he said.

For some reason known only to himself, Colonel Vivian blushed.

SIX: THE LAST PERFORMANCE

CHAPTER ONE

The last forty-eight hours had been confusing for Trepper, very confusing indeed. Not only was he puzzled as to how the Germans had known so much about his movements that they could be waiting for him at the dentist's, he was also bewildered by their behaviour. Immediately after his arrest, he had been taken to the notorious Fresnes Prison and flung into solitary. That he had expected. It was standard operating procedure on the part of the Gestapo. Let a prisoner stew in his own juice for a while to soften him up before they started to work on him. What had happened next – or better, what hadn't happened – had not been expected. He had not been called from his cell for the first grilling.

'Why not?' he asked himself, his big face set in a look of bewilderment.

Surely they would want to work him over immediately to get the names of his other agents before they took a dive? But instead of the grilling he anticipated, the next morning when the warder flung open his cell-door, he was served an ample breakfast, including a precious egg, given a razor and a bowl of hot water and was ordered to shave and wash. Half an hour later he was in a three-engined Junkers transport on his way to Berlin.

All that afternoon, and late into the night, his bewilderment increasing by the hour. His cell in the basement of the *Prinzalbrechtstrasse* Gestapo H.Q. was visited by a succession of notables, who came in to stare at him as if he were some strange wild beast, found in captivity for the very first time. He recognised Himmler, and Goering, and later on Stahl came in with a man named Mueller, a small, hooded-eyed officer with the square head of a peasant. Later he discovered that the man was no other than 'Gestapo' Mueller, the head of the dreaded Secret Police!

Now in this third day, still ungrilled and completely puzzled by his quite unexpected treatment, he was back in Paris. But not in Fresnes. Instead he was lodged in an improvised cell in the *Abwehr* H.Q. in the Rue de Saussaies. It was extremely comfortable – they had even provided him with an armchair – and the sympathetic-looking captain with one arm had brought him some fruit and a novel by Colette to read. But Trepper was unable to concentrate on the silly goings-on of Gigi; his mind was too preoccupied with the strange treatment he was being afforded. What the devil had the Fritzes in store for him? So far he had not revealed to them that he spoke German, but in spite of straining his ears till they hurt to pick up the slightest piece of information regarding his fate, he was still without a clue.

About six that evening, the tall, ill-looking Gestapo man with the hoarse voice, who had arrested him – the one they called Stahl – entered, followed by the one-armed captain. The Gestapo officer put two cups on the table, told the fat NCO to pour coffee into them from the steaming hot pot he was holding, and then added two generous slugs of cognac out of the silver flask he produced from his pocket. He pushed one cup towards the prisoner and said, '*A votre santé!*' He raised his cup in toast.

'*A la votre!*' Trepper raised his and took a cautious sip, wondering if the Gestapo man was feeding him some sort of truth drug.

Then almost immediately he dismissed the suggestion as absurd. Stahl was drinking the same mixture himself.

Peipe told Fat Heinz to leave and sat himself down to the left of the two men at the table so that he could observe the spymaster's reaction from the side, as he had agreed to do with Stahl.

For a while Stahl chatted with the conductor in his poor French, helped out by Peipe, while both men took stock of each other like two animals sniffing out strengths and weaknesses.

Once the Gestapo man said, 'In Berlin, people are beginning to count the rivers between them and the Front, now that your people have reached the Dnieper.'

Trepper said, 'It reminds me of the anecdote about the Kaiser in 1918 when he told one of his generals he was impatient to reach the Front. To which the general replied, "Never fear your Majesty. It won't be long before the Front reaches you."'

Stahl looked at him curiously, but there was sudden hard light in his faded eyes. 'You think so?'

Trepper realised he had gone too far – after all this was a senior Gestapo official he was dealing with – and he added hastily. 'Oh, rivers! First they flow one way and then the other.' It was a meaningless phrase, but it seemed to soothe the German.

They chatted for hours, while the clock ticked metallically on the wall. The black-out curtains were drawn. Outside, the volume of traffic decreased and died away altogether. Now it was curfew. But still nothing was said which could give an increasingly nervous and puzzled Trepper a clue as to the Germans' intentions. The Gestapo man's French, thick, guttural and inaccurate, started to irritate him. In the end Trepper's nerves got the better of him and he forced the situation. Suddenly he announced, while Stahl filled his cup with yet more cognac, '*Sie können mir ruhig ein wenig einschenken. Das Bisschen haut mich night um.*'*

Stahl looked at him, startled. 'So you speak German, too, eh?' He flashed a quick look at Peipe, who nodded back. He had recognised the accent, too. After all he had heard it often enough in Berlin before 1933. It was the accent of the Yiddish speaker.

Stahl finished pouring the cognac and said, 'You're a Jew, aren't you?'

'Yes,' Trepper said, outwardly quite calm, though his nerves were jingling, now that he had given himself away.

Stahl was silent for a moment. Then he said: 'Well, my dear friend, you really are in a fix. A spy, a Communist, and now a Jew to boot. You are certainly loading on the misery.'

Trepper said nothing. He had made an opening gambit. He could tell by the look on the other man's face that the chat was over; the real game would begin soon.

All the same, Stahl's own opening gambit puzzled him: 'You know that you've lost, not only against us, but against your Centre in Moscow?'

Trepper chose to remain silent, wondering frantically what the Gestapo man meant by the last part of his announcement.

'Of course, you think we've got you here to knock out the names of the rest of the Orchestra from your body.' Stahl shook his head. 'Not one bit. We're not interested. They're just small fry, anyway.'

'I bet you still don't have the pianist,' Trepper ventured.

'No, I admit we don't? But what good is a pianist without an Orchestra or a conductor, eh?' Stahl turned to Peipe. 'Captain, I'm getting hoarse. You read out the list.'

While Stahl sipped his cognac moodily, Peipe read out a list of names and addresses, concluding with the words, 'Those men and women we have already arrested.'

* 'You can give me a bit more. That little bit won't hurt me.'

Trepper cursed to himself. Vasili had known more than he had thought. The damned emigré had sung like a canary, that was obvious. But there was worse to come.

Looking at him over the edge of the paper, Captain Peipe said: 'This is a list of names and addresses of those members of your Orchestra that we still have not arrested.' Thereupon he read out the names of a dozen or more members of the Paris, Lyons and Amsterdam networks.

For what seemed a long time there was a dead silence, broken only by the heavy solemn tick-tock of the wall clock. Finally Stahl broke it. 'You see, my dear Herr Trepper, we don't really need you to wipe out the rest of your network. In fact the small fry don't interest us in the least. We have a much more important objective.'

'Yes,' Peipe butted in, as agreed. 'We must bring this disastrous war to an end between our two countries. In the end, who will benefit from this war? The Anglo-Americans. Those plutocrats are only waiting for our two nations to drain each other dry, before they step in to pick up the loot.'

Trepper nodded his head slightly, as if he were agreeing, though he knew in his own mind that the Gestapo man did not mean one word of what he had just said.

'Now we would like you, Herr Trepper, to help us in the task of trying to achieve peace between our two nations.' Peipe went on before Trepper could ask what particular role he was supposed to play in the monumental task. 'Now obviously you can refuse to help us. Frankly it wouldn't worry us very much. You see, we are already in contact with Moscow, and we can start talking to them without your help. But with you, it would be better.' He nodded to Stahl to take over.

There was iron in the Gestapo man's hoarse voice when he spoke now. 'Let me put it to you straight, Trepper. If you refuse to co-operate, you'll die twice – in a manner of speaking. Here we'd shoot you as a spy. Then we'll make Moscow believe you turned traitor and went over to us, revealing the names of your agents in a vain attempt to save your own head. You know we can do that. At the Centre, as you know well, they are always suspicious of their men in the field. As soon as you fellows leave on operations, you are already suspected as potential defectors or turncoats.'

Trepper's heart sank. He knew the Gestapo man was right. The Director, and Stalin his boss, had little faith in their agents, once they couldn't be supervised by Russian counter-intelligence. Hadn't Sorge's* warning, from Japan in '41, that Germany was about to invade the Soviet Union, been completely ignored? Indeed, Stalin had ordered the agent punished for spreading rumours. Yet he knew he must not show his despondency to his captors; they would only take advantage of it. His best defence, he knew, was attack.

'Let's cut out the crap, shall we?' he snarled suddenly.

Stahl tapped his forehead with his forefinger. 'Are you *meschugge*, talking to a member of the Gestapo like that, you crazy Kike?'

Trepper ignored the outburst. Instead, he leaned forward across the table, his eyes blazing with forced anger, though inside he quaked with fear of what might happen to him, if his attack failed to hit home.

'Now listen, Stahl, or whatever your name is. You're not interested one bit in a peace between Russia and Germany. You are a patriotic, loyal German. Your one aim is to destroy Russia and you want me to help you to do so,' he shouted.

Stahl opened his mouth to say something, but Trepper didn't give him a chance. He could see from the look on the man's face that his attack was succeeding. He pressed on with it. 'I know exactly why you've brought me here, given me books and food, why I was taken to Berlin, and why you haven't had me down in your torture cellars yet.' His big chest heaved with the effort of speaking so rapidly and he gasped for breath.

Peipe took advantage of the slight pause. Swiftly he asked, 'Why?'

'Why?' Trepper sneered, flashing him a look of contempt. 'It is as plain as the fact that you have only got one flipper.' Peipe flushed. 'Because you want me to play the radio game with Moscow, that's why.' Trepper stopped and glared at their surprised faces, as if challenging them to deny that he was right . . .

CHAPTER TWO

It was now well past midnight. After his outburst, Trepper had allowed Stahl to give him another cognac, and had listened in silence while Stahl had outlined the radio game that 'Gestapo' Mueller, in Berlin, had ordered should be played with the Director of the Moscow Centre. In essence, as Stahl ex-

* The Russian spymaster in Japan.

plained it, he, Trepper, would be saved from the executioner's axe, if he agreed to resume his messages to Moscow. Only this time, the conductor, the Orchestra and the pianist would be German, the aim being to send carefully-prepared false information to Moscow, not only of a military nature, but also political, intended to spread dissension between Russia and her Western Allies.

As Stahl summed it up, 'It's co-operation or death, Trepper. And I'll ensure personally – if I live that long – that you are given a new identity and money to make a fresh start in a neutral country when the war is over. Now what do you say?' With that he leaned back in his chair, cup cradled in his claw-like hands.

Trepper forced himself to play it cool. 'It won't work, you know,' he said after a long moment's pause. 'I might be prepared to co-operate – I'm not saying I will – but even if I did, do you think you could keep a radio game of that nature hidden from Moscow for long?'

'What do you mean?' Peipe asked hotly.

'You underestimate my masters in Moscow. My Orchestra was quite good, but it was nothing in comparison with the counter-intelligence system the Director set up to protect it and keep an eye on it.'

The two Germans looked impressed, and Trepper continued with growing confidence. 'It is everywhere and all-powerful. It'll find out that I'm your prisoner soon enough and inform Moscow. Then what, eh?' He sniffed contemptuously. 'Then your fine radio game will be in the bucket.' He paused and waited for their reaction, although he had already decided what he was going to do.

Thus the battle of wits continued, until a hollow-eyed, weary Peipe drew back the black-out curtains to reveal the dawn. They had talked all night long. Nothing had really been decided. He, Trepper, had not refused outright to collaborate; he had only pointed out the futility of doing so. Stahl and Peipe, for their parts, had not insisted that he collaborate. That would have undermined their assertion that they could do without Trepper in the planned radio game.

Peipe yawned, and said wearily, 'I'm going to hit the sack. I've had enough for this day.'

Stahl eyed the two empty bottles of cognac and yawned his agreement.

Trepper, confident, now that he was the master of the situation, and as clear-headed as ever, ventured one last question. 'By the way, Herr Stahl, may I ask you how you got on to me in the first place?'

Groggily Stahl staggered to his feet and answered in a thick croak, 'You just got careless, I suppose.'

Trepper nodded his head sagely. 'Yes, I suppose I did.'

But when they had left, and the fat NCO had fixed a notice on his door reading 'Special Prisoner – Keep Out!', Trepper could not go to sleep, in spite of his weariness. '*Careless*,' he asked himself time and time again, turning over on the narrow bed. '*How careless . . . how?*'

One week after that conversation, Trepper was transferred to a new prison: a private house somewhere. He found it a charming house, with a façade of Greek columns and a large garden, in which he was allowed to exercise daily under the watchful eyes of polite Slovak guards, who spoke neither French nor German. For the time being, while he took stock of his surroundings, Trepper decided not to approach them in Russian or Polish, which they might well understand. Instead, he noted the high railings around the large garden which had been covered with black galvanised sheeting to block out the view, though from the sound of the pedestrians strolling beyond, he concluded that there were no sentries on the far side of them.

During the first days in the strange house – he suspected that there were other prisoners there, too – he spent many an hour staring out of his tall barred window at the grey Gothic steeple of a distant church, and a few seedy horses and carriages he could just make out by standing on a chair. He was trying to locate his prison. In the end he came to the conclusion he was in one of the remoter, but wealthier Parisian suburbs – hence the horses – Neuilly, perhaps, in which it would be more than difficult for him to disappear quickly if he could succeed in getting over the rails, past the Slovak sentries. In other words, he would have to play ball with the Germans in order to put himself in a more favourable position to effect an escape and warn the Centre what was afoot. For his talk of a tremendous Russian counter-intelligence *apparat* in France had been all hot air. There was no such thing.

On February 1st, 1943, Trepper pretended to bow to the inevitable, although he had long accepted the inevitablity of working with the Germans; it was the only way, he knew, to escape from his prison. He asked to see Stahl and find out his terms.

Instead, the one-armed Captain Peipe appeared in Stahl's place. After explaining that Stahl had had a collapse and was presently in the Paris Military Hospital, Peipe said: 'I'm authorised to act in his place. I have the full confidence of General Mueller. Now, Trepper, what's on your mind?'

Trepper lowered his eyes and gave an eloquent shrug of defeat. 'You fellers have got me by the short hairs,' he said a little despondently. 'I'll co-operate.'

Peipe looked at the former conductor keenly. 'Remember, Trepper no tricks,' he said, 'or it'll be much worse for you.'

Trepper raised his head and with a look of fear in his dark eyes, he said: 'You don't have to worry about tricks from me, Captain. I know what would happen to me, if I tried to betray you. Your friends of the Gestapo would soon see they'd put me up the chimney.' He made the spiralling gesture of smoke ascending into the sky, the symbol of the concentration-camp ovens. 'I'm a Jew, after all. I'll play fair and square.'

'All right, Trepper,' Peipe said, feeling a little sorry for the once powerful spymaster, now obviously completely broken and dispirited. 'I'll inform General Mueller of your decision immediately.'

Thereafter things happened swiftly. The other prisoners in the house were moved out, to be replaced by members of his own Orchestra, including the Maximovs, and Wenzel, the pianist of the Dutch part of his Orchestra. A new jailer from the Berlin Gestapo appeared to take Stahl's place: a fat, undersized, bald Gestapo man named Berg. Trepper got on with him famously. The man lived solely for booze and jokes. His three children had been killed in one of the Berlin air raids and his wife had gone crazy as a result; Berg was a broken man, whose sole concern was to forget the war.

In the second week of February, Wenzel sent his first message to Moscow under Trepper's direction. Unknown to Trepper, Peipe had ordered the message should be transmitted into the void. In other words, their message never reached Moscow. Instead it was recorded and examined minutely by German experts, whose job it was to detect any change in the pianist's 'fist', or any trick that might have warned Moscow. After forty-eight hours of intensive examination, the experts pronounced the message 'clean'. Trepper and Wenzel were living up to their part of the bargain. Peipe ordered that the pianist should now be allowed to contact the Centre in earnest.

After several days of trying, they finally picked up a message from the Centre. It read: 'What has happened? Why no transmission?'

Even Trepper, the forced double-agent, seemed pleased, or so it seemed to Peipe, that contact had finally been made. He even suggested that the prepared German answer should contain some reference to the arrests, but should confirm that the network was still intact. Peipe agreed. One night later the pianist signalled: 'Some confusion due to several arrests. Now everything all right once again.'

The Centre bought the signal.

As February gave way to March, the new Orchestra settled down and started performing, as if they really enjoyed the new concert. The relationship between the captives and their captors which had begun in mutual distrust developed into a form of comradeship. The two groups talked shop all day long, sharing the same meals, drinking the same drinks, exchanging jokes, in a strange limbo, as if this remote, guarded suburban villa was the real world, outside of which nothing else existed.

Peipe, half-amused, half-suspicious, noted that Trepper had developed a very warm relationship with his chief jailer, the fat tubby Gestapo-man, Berg, pulling his leg about his figure and the inevitable vinegar-soaked bandage he wore around his bald head to ease the pain of the headache which was the result of the previous night's drinking. He told himself he'd better keep an eye on 'Fat Willy', as the dying Stahl called him.

But Stahl shook his head weakly, when he had reported his suspicions to the Gestapo-man. 'No, Peipe, my friend,' he had croaked, his throat now almost eaten away by the killer disease, 'you can trust Willy. I've known him for years. He's a professional cop like me.' Stahl, lying shrunken in the white metal bed, tried to shrug, but failed miserably. 'If Willy's getting friendly with the Yid, he's doing it for his own purposes, believe you me.'

In the second week of March, Peipe received 'Gestapo' Mueller's order, via Admiral Canaris's office in the *Tirpitzstrasse,* to carry the great deception game a stage further. That day he consulted his brief from Mueller, which emphasized that the 'best of alliances is never very far from separation or even divorce', and stated explicitly that the chief aim of the radio game was to split the Western Allies and the Russians by inflaming their mutual suspicions.

That evening he called Trepper to him, and after the exchange of a few pleasantries about his new role as double-agent, launched into the details of the second stage, his eyes watching the conductor's face all the time for any clue to his real feelings.

'In essence, Trepper, he announced, 'we have set up this operation in order to be able to open up negotiations with your Russian masters. I mean, it is not difficult to get into touch with the Western Allies. We Germans and they, both have embassies in neutral capitals everywhere – Stockholm, Madrid, Ankara. You Russians don't have those embassies. Therefore it's up to you and your pianist.'

Trepper eyed him cynically. 'My dear Captain, please put your cards on the table. I can guess what your real intention is. You want to play off the West against the East to the advantage of your own country. If I am to conduct the Orchestra well, I must know the score, you know.'

Peipe looked at him for a long time. 'Am I so transparent, Trepper?' he asked.

Trepper smiled gently. 'No, Captain. But I have been in this business all my adult life. In comparison, you are a novice. Besides,' he tapped his nose, 'I've got a big enough beak to be able to sniff out a fake.' The conductor took the liberty of reaching forward and patting Peipe's knee gently. 'No matter, Captain, I am completely in your power. I will do as you wish, only I hope you will be completely honest with me. I can do a better job of work that way.'

Trepper seemed to be completely genuine. With only nominal supervision from Fat Willy, he sent message after message prepared by Mueller's experts in Berlin, designed to make Moscow suspicious of Anglo-American intentions, now that Russia was obviously winning the war.

According to a doctored Berlin account, wounded British and American airmen hospitalised at Clichy Military Hospital had stated to Orchestra agents that they were fed up with the war: the real enemy was Russia, not Germany. Other agents reported that Calais, the centre of German defences against an invasion from Britain, was swarming with German troops, armed with Sten-guns. But where had the Germans obtained the British-manufactured weapons? Moscow demanded urgently. Dutifully the pianist signalled back that they had been purchased in a neutral country, obviously (so Moscow was meant to think) with British connivance.

Berlin took the great game a little further. That April the pianist signalled the Centre that Sir Samuel Hoare, the right-wing British ambassador to Madrid, had met German Foreign Minister and former German ambassador to London, Joachim von Ribbentrop, somewhere in Spain, for confidential talks.

As Peipe read the flood of messages before passing them on to Berg, he could not but admire the ingenuity of the Berlin group which prepared them. Brick upon brick, Berlin was building up a wall of suspicion between the West and East. He could well imagine what Stalin was thinking. The Western Allies were sitting on their well-fed arses in Britain, not lifting a finger to fight the war, while they waited calmly (as the saying of the time had it) for 'the last Russian soldier to kill the last German soldier'.

Trepper was keeping his word. The conductor had the Orchestra well under control.

That same spring, Peipe visited Stahl for the last time. His long lean frame was wasted down to virtually nothing. The bed behind the screen in which he lay seemed empty; there was so little of him left.

Embarrassed, a little helpless, Peipe stared down at the cop's grey skull-face, the expressionless eyes sunk deep, deep into the bones.

'So this is how it ends,' he told himself. All his life, Stahl had been a cop, believing in nothing in particular, especially not in that creature called Man. Year in, year out, serving masters in uniforms of different hues, whom he despised, he had inhabited a remote cynical world of grey offices and dirty tiled corridors, snatching hasty lunches of greasy sandwiches, washed down with warm beer, adjusting his face, his thoughts, his words to each new prisoner. All those long dreary grey years he had not subscribed to any moral code, believing himself the representative of right and the prisoner, the representative of wrong. He had done his job strictly, because he wanted to make his prisoner 'sing' (his favourite word) and have him sentenced, so that he could go on to the next sordid case.

And now he was dying, alone and unmourned. Not even his boss, 'Gestapo' Mueller, had enquired about him since he had been delivered into the Clichy Hospital.

Stahl's eyes flickered open and with great exertion, he forced a smile. 'I was a good cop,' he croaked in a faint, faint whisper. 'That's why they're glad to get rid of me,' he said, as if he had read Peipe's mind.

Peipe tried to smile, and indicated the flowers and the bottle of fine cognac he had brought. 'Your medicine,' he said.

Stahl didn't seem to notice. 'I wasn't like you fine gents of the *Abwehr*, believing in God . . . or those rats of the SS, who put their faith in the Devil . . . I was just a cop . . . They didn't like that.' He gave a great gasp and Peipe's nostrils were assailed by the nauseating stink of death that came from his toothless mouth.

'Now, don't say that, Stahl,' he said hastily. 'That medicine of yours—'

Weakly, Stahl held up a claw of a hand to stop him. 'Let me give you a piece of advice, Peipe,' he croaked in a cracked whisper.

Overcoming his nausea at the stench of rotting flesh, Peipe leaned forward so that he could hear. 'Get out, Peipe!'

'Get out?'

'Out of this business, Peipe,' Stahl whispered in a voice so faint now that Peipe had to turn his head to catch the words. 'Let that Yid get on with it. His type always lands on his feet. People like Fat Willy won't survive anyway. But you'll swing, Peipe.'

'Swing?'

Stahl cackled, pink-coloured spittle gathering at the edges of his cracked, bitten lips. 'At the end of a rope, Peipe,' he explained, with just a trace of his old bitter humour. 'We've lost, Peipe – the war. And if you don't get out of the Orchestra now, you'll swing at the end of a Russian rope when they get here, which they surely will.' He coughed thickly and wiped away the blood with his skinny hand. 'Get out of the Orchestra, while there's still time, Peipe.' His hand fell listlessly to the sheet, staining it bright red with blood. 'Now get out of here and let me die in peace.' He closed his eyes, and after a while Peipe tip-toed out.

Two days later Stahl died in his sleep. Peipe and Willy Berg, drunk as usual, were the only two present at his funeral. When Willy tried to take off 'Gestapo' Mueller's wreath, a small one, from the coffin, he staggered alarmingly and almost fell into the open grave. One week later Admiral Canaris approved

Peipe's transfer to Colonel Giskes' counter-intelligence unit operating against the British in Holland. The Gestapo had no objections. They were glad to see him go. Mueller wanted the kudos of the great radio game to go to the Gestapo.

Thus is was that Peipe lived to see the end of the war. Apart from the conductor, he would be the only one to do so, just as the dying Stahl had predicted...

CHAPTER THREE

Trepper was bothered, very bothered. It was now nearly six months since he had agreed to work for the Germans, and in spite of his and Wenzel's attempts to indicate to the Centre that they were working under duress, Moscow had failed to understand their carefully planted tips. It was obvious that Moscow was buying the radio game.

But that wasn't the only thing that worried the conductor, as the long days passed, that summer in the secluded villa, and there was still no indication from the Director that he realised that the Orchestra was really being conducted by the Fritzes. Over the months he had considered how he had been captured. The dead Gestapo officer had said it had been due to his carelessness. But how had he been careless? His external security had been excellent and his choice of agents had been virtually fool-proof save for the unfortunate Jeanette – and he had soon rectified that fault.

But where had the Fritzes obtained his photograph, the one Maximov had mentioned, that had been circulated to all the German units in *Gross-Paris*? It was clear to him now that it had come from someone within the organisation. How, too, had the Germans been able to pick out Vasili from the hundreds of German and foreign officers who frequented the Hotel Majestic? Obviously, again from a tip-off from within the Orchestra. But who was the traitor?

Trepper ran his mind over the faces, the backgrounds, the actions of the many scores of agents in half-a-dozen countries who had made up the Orchestra. Day after day, week after week, month after month, he pondered over that overwhelming question: *Who*?

And then it came to him in a moment of total, absolute recall. '*Don't forget your choppers,*' he had said in that bantering, yet mocking voice of his. '*It can be hell to have toothache when you've gone underground. I know. It happened to me when I took a dive in '41.'*

Trepper clicked his fingers excitedly. *The Belgian; of course, it had to be the Belgian – the damned pianist*!

That same evening, when Willy was well into his second bottle of cheap *Korn*, his fat face a crimson-red, Trepper broached the subject casually, smiling in that soft understanding manner of his, which made him '*sehr sympathisch*' to the roly-poly Gestapo man.

Willy grinned back at him, swaying a little in his chair. 'Trying to pump me, when I'm in my cups, eh, Trepper?' he said thickly, wagging a finger like a sausage in front of the Conductor's nose. 'Naughty, naughty!'

'Did I ever tell you the joke of the Jew who hadn't been circumcised and the Party doctor?' Trepper changed the subject quickly, and began telling one of the dirty jokes Willy loved.

But half an hour and three *Korns* later, he returned to the subject of how he had been finally trapped; and this time Willy, by now completely drunk, did not withold the information from him.

'According to poor old Stahli,' he said thickly, 'they found some sort of calling card with the name of your dentist on it, Trepper. Now what do you say to that?'

For once Trepper had nothing to say. Instead he launched into yet another smutty joke, his face wreathed in a broad smile. But there was rage and hate in his heart.

Now he had a double reason for getting out. He must warn Moscow – and he must deal with the traitor!

On Friday the 13th of September, 1943, Willy awoke with a shocking headache. That wasn't anything unusual with him. But the night before he had celebrated more than usual, if that was the correct word for his night-long binge. For the 12th September was the anniversary of his children's death and the day his wife had gone mad.

At midday, he arrived at the villa, racked with pain, his head wrapped in the usual vinegar-soaked bandage, which didn't go well with his uniformed cap, adorned with the frightening death's-head of the SS. 'Oh, my aching arse, Trepper!' he had groaned, when Trepper had wished him good morning. 'I think my shitting turnip is going to fall off!'

'Isn't the bandage doing you any good?'

'The only good it's doing, is keeping my head on my shoulders. I've got the father and mother of all shitty headaches. I think I'm going to snuff it.'

Trepper laughed. 'Now, now, it can't be that bad.'

'Oh, yes, it can. It's worse! I've tried beer, coffee, schnapps – and about half a ton of aspirin. Nothing shitting-well works!'

'You remember that pharmacy I once told you about – near the Gare St Lazare?' Berg's answer was a pitiful moan. 'They sell a remedy there against headaches which works wonders. I know. I've bought it a few times in the past. It could cure an elephant's headache.'

Willy, holding his head in both hands, looked up at him with red eyes. 'Do you really think so?'

'Of course,' Trepper said, full of confidence. 'Let me buy you it. That headache of yours will be gone in a quarter of an hour. But we'll need the car.'

'We'll get it,' Willy answered with renewed hope. He picked up the phone and completely missed the new look in Trepper's face.

Five minutes later, with Willy and a solicitous Trepper sitting in the back, the chauffeur-driven black Peugeot was threading its way through the mid-day traffic towards the *Pharmacie Bailly.*

The car came to a halt in the Rue de Rome, on the western side of the busy railway station. It was now the noon rush hour. With a sigh of relief Trepper noted there were people and vehicles everywhere. It was just what he wanted. As the car-driver turned off his engine opposite the pharmacy's main entrance, he gazed up at the huge drugstore, with its counters and laboratories spread over two floors. Bailly's looked very busy, too. People were hurrying in and out of the building. That was also all to the good.

Swiftly he got out and opened the door.

Willy struggled out, and stood there on the pavement, swaying wildly. 'But there are several doors into the place,' he protested weakly.

Trepper answered brightly, with more confidence than he felt. 'Naturally. But you're coming in with me, Willy, aren't you?' He knew now that even if he had to tackle Willy physically, he would get away with it. The Gestapo man was in a terrible state; it would be a walk-over.

Berg hesitated, and then slumped back into his seat weakly.

'Oh, never mind my coming, Trepper. I can trust you. But for God's sake, get me that cure quickly. My head's about to explode!'

Trepper hesitated no longer. 'Won't be a minute,' he said, and forcing himself to take his time, he sauntered into the overcrowded store.

Once inside, he wasted no time. Roughly he elbowed his way through the pale-faced women waiting for their prescriptions at the long counter, ignoring their protests. What did he care about them? It was only their toes or ribs that were being hurt. His life was at stake. He fought his way through to the Rue de Rocher on the other side of the store.

Now there was no time to be lost. By now Willy would have missed him. Perhaps he was already walking into the *Pharmacie* himself, to check what had happened to him. Perhaps he had ordered his driver to telephone the nearest Gestapo post. Within minutes they would be there in the black Citroens, cordoning off all exits, checking papers, arresting people. Trying not to run, but making the best speed possible without arousing the suspicion of the gendarmes posted outside the station, he walked swiftly up the Rue d'Amsterdam and jumped in the first train leaving the station. It went to St Germain-en-Laye. He waited there for thirty minutes. Knowing that there would be one place where the Gestapo would *not* be looking for him, he spent the last of his money taking the *metro* and bus back to St Lazare. When he got out, the Gestapo had gone and the *Pharmacie* was back to normal. Trepper sighed with relief. Soon it would be dusk and curfew. He was on the run in Paris, with not a sou to his name, and (so it appeared) every man's hand against him.

CHAPTER FOUR

It was now dusk. In an hour it would be curfew, and a frantic Trepper knew that he must be under cover by then. But where? Since he had been arrested, six months ago, the contacts he had had, had been either apprehended by the Boche, or had taken a dive. At that moment, he could not think of one single way of making contact with the underground French Communist Party, which he knew would help him. By now he was hungry, thirsty and very weary. He had circled the station time and time again, mingling with the crowds, knowing that a lounger invariably attracted attention, and his feet were sore.

Thus he committed what was for him a rash act. During his time as managing-director of Simex, Malepate, the dentist, had advised him to take a series of injections for his health, and had recommended a nurse to do the job: a simple, kindly, middle-aged spinster, whose family name he had forgotten, though he remembered he had addressed her as Lucie.

He knew even as he started to limp towards her house that he was taking a great risk. Malepate might have given her address to the Boche. But that wasn't all. She lived in the Rue de Surene, just off the German Intelligence HQ at the Rue des Saussaies. But as if that weren't enough, the house she inhabited also contained the offices of the French pro-Nazi Party, the *Rassemblement National Populaire*, and there was always an armed guard on duty at the entrance!

Yet as he passed the wooden-faced French sentry, who didn't even look at this footsore, shabby, unshaven civilian, Trepper told himself that perhaps, after all, his calculated risk might yet pay off. Who would suspect the hunted spymaster would try to find refuge from his hunters only a mere hundred metres from their HQ?

He tramped up the dark stairs to the nurse's flat, rehearsing what he would say to her. He knew he must not tell her he was a spy on the run. That would certainly frighten her off; she would think he was too big a fish for her to hide. He must think of something else. Just as he rang the bell, glancing nervously over his shoulder at the open door and the wooden-faced sentry below, he had it.

A pleasant, middle-aged woman, with her greying hair swept back from her homely face, opened the door, and recognised him immediately, although she had not seen him for nearly a year. 'What a surprise, Monsieur Gilbert –'

He didn't give her a chance to finish. Instead, he whispered urgently, 'Listen, M'selle Lucie, you didn't know it when I came here that time, but I'm a Jew. I've just escaped from a German camp and I'm on the run. Can you hide me for a couple of days?' He pressed his hand to his heart, as if he might be seriously ill.

To his surprise, the middle-aged nurse burst into tears. For a moment, his heart sank. She was scared, she wasn't going to help him, he told himself in sudden panic.

But to his relief she choked through her sobs, 'Of course I'll help you, Monsieur Gilbert . . . Come on in, quick!'

Trepper needed no urging. He stepped inside swiftly and slumped down on the nearest chair, exhausted. He had done it; he had escaped!

The next forty-eight hours Trepper spent in the nurse's flat, his only activity watching the coming and goings of the Gestapo's black, discreet Citroens from the Rue des Saussaies HQ. He had noted the cars' numbers long ago when he had been a prisoner in the remote suburban villa.

On the third day he came to the conclusion that there was no unusual activity – which surprised him – at the Gestapo HQ. He decided to venture out into the streets for the first time since he had escaped. Waiting till Lucie had set off on her daily rounds as a private nurse, he slipped out past the sentry into the streets, carrying the paper and the long loaf of bread Lucie had brought in for his breakfast, under his arm, as if he were the typical mid-morning stroller.

But his casual pose soon vanished when he passed the police station in the Rue de Surene. There, plastered for all to see on both sides of the entrance, was his own photograph, blown up to many times its normal size, with the bold words printed below it: '*Very dangerous spy. Escaped! A reward will be paid for information leading to his capture.*'

Turning up his collar, as if he were protecting his throat against the November cold, Trepper dropped his pose of the casual stroller. Hurriedly he made his way back to the nurse's flat, his now very well-known face hidden in the pages of the newspaper as he passed the immobile sentry in his blue uniform. Once upstairs, he flung the loaf full force against the wall. It was a rare outburst of temper on his part – he had learned to control himself many years ago – but at that particular moment he was exasperated beyond measure.

But soon he would learn there was worse to come. On the fourth day after his escape, as he was burning with impatience to contact someone who would be able to inform Moscow what was going on in that lonely suburban villa, he took Lucie a little into his confidence.

'Now listen,' he said carefully, pressing her reddened, work-worn hand, for she was an emotional woman, given often to tears, 'I don't want you to worry. But I'm more than just a Jew on the run.' She nodded. 'I am also working for the Allies – for victory and freedom.' Again the middle-aged nurse nodded, but said nothing. 'Now I would like you to do me a favour. My friends of the – er – Resistance will want to know where I am.'

'But isn't that –'

'No, it isn't dangerous,' he beat her to it. 'Not for you anyway. All you have to do is to pass this piece of paper on to a friend. Look, read it yourself and you'll see how harmless it is.'

He handed her the pencil-scribbled note and she put on her gold-rimmed spectacles. her most precious possession, to read it aloud: '*Conductor at liberty for work. Can you suggest new place of appointment?*'

She looked up at him blankly. 'What does it mean?' she asked.

'You see?' he said triumphantly. 'You don't understand one word of it. And it would be the same if the Gestapo stopped you', he lied. 'They wouldn't be able to make head or tail of it.'

'And where do I take it?' she asked, replacing her spectacles in their case, carefully, obviously convinced.

'To this address,' Trepper said hastily. 'Now I'm not going to write it down. You'll have to memorize it. All right?'

'*D'accord,*' the trusting nurse answered, obviously puzzled by the whole business, yet trying to help as she had helped all her life.

Trepper knew that it was a long shot. But he knew no other way of contacting the C.P. The man's name had come to him on the morning of the fourth day, as he had lain, tossing and turning in his narrow bed, wondering what he should do next. It was Charles Lederman, a lawyer who was a member of the Jewish Resistance movement. Normally he had no time for fellow Jews who dabbled in Zionism; hadn't Stalin himself said that Zionism was as bad as Fascism? But this particular Jew was also in touch with Kovalsky, the Communist Resistance leader, who in his turn, reported to the leaders of the Communist *Francs-Tireurs et Partisans*, and the great partisan movement was under the direct control of the Central Committee of the French Communist Party. It was, he knew, a very roundabout way of making contact, but there was no other means available to him, and he was desperate.

'The name is Lederman,' he said. 'The man is a lawyer, and he's got an office in the Rue de l'Hachette. Go there and give him the paper. He'll understand.'

But Lederman's answer was a disappointment and a shock. From the look on Lucie's homely red face, Trepper knew that something had gone wrong even before she handed him back the note she had taken to the Jewish lawyer. He opened it curiously. Neatly printed in a small legal hand on the back of his own message, there was one single word. It read '*Traitor.*'

Now, some hours later, nursing the second brandy that a bewildered, anxious Lucie had brought him after he had collapsed into the chair, his face blanched with shock, Trepper could understand what had happened. It would have been the same sort of trick he would have pulled himself. Willy, or whoever was running the radio game now, so he had decided, had obviously made use of the second pianist they had established in Lyons three months before, who worked apparently independently of the Paris Orchestra. The Lyons pianist had probably sent a supposedly innocent message, reading: 'What has happened to Trepper? I see 'Wanted' notices for him everywhere. Has he escaped from a Fritz prison?'

In Moscow the shit would certainly have hit the fan. There a furious and obviously highly embarrassed Director would have immediately reasoned that Trepper had been working for the enemy ever since the Paris Orchestra had resumed transmissions since the break. In other words, Paris had been involved in a radio game for the last six months or so. Trepper knew, only too well, what his reaction would have been. An order would have flashed out to all organisations. '*Avoid Trepper like the plague. He is a traitor.*' Sitting there in his chair, the pale-faced conductor shivered violently in spite of the fiery spirit which was trickling down his gullet at that particular moment. Not only that, he told himself fearfully, another order would have followed the first. It would have read in the simple, brutal style of the Beria's HQ*: '*Liquidate Trepper!*'

That evening he made his decision. He knew now he was between the devil and the deep blue sea. He could not go backwards – only forwards. Breaking the long heavy silence at last, he said to Lucie, who had watched him all evening, her bovine face set in a look of concern, 'Lucie, I've stayed here long enough.'

'No, no, Monsieur Gilbert!' she protested. 'You don't need to go, whatever the bad news was you received today. I can hide you – and if the rations are not so good, we'll survive.'

He squeezed her hand, a warm smile on his face, but his eyes

* The feared head of the Soviet Secret Police.

cold. He had always been able to use people, thank God, he told himself, and this silly old cow was no exception.

'No, that is expecting too much from you, Lucie,' he said. 'Winter is coming on and it's going to be a hard one. But you can give me a little money and some sandwiches to last the next twenty-four hours. Could you do that for me – one last kindness?'

'Of course, of course,' she cried, already beginning to sob in her excessive emotional way.

One hour later he was ready to go, taking a chance of being caught out in the curfew, but knowing the darkness would hide his face. In his pocket he had all her remaining bread and sausage and most of her pathetic savings. He pressed her hand warmly, and told himself, 'Oh, stop howling, you silly old bag.' To her face, he said, however, 'I shall never forget you, Lucie. Thank you!'

'And I will never forget you too, M'sieur Gilbert . . . *Bonne chance!*' she whispered fervently through her tears; and she never did, until that day in March 1945, when they came to take her for her last walk to the ovens in Dachau.

Trepper had forgotten the nurse before he reached the bottom of the stairs . . .

CHAPTER FIVE

Trepper grabbed Lederman by the lapels of his flamboyant silken dressing-gown and slammed him against the wall before he could close the door of his apartment.

'Listen,' he grunted, keeping the frightened, dark-faced lawyer pinned to the wall, while from inside the apartment his wife's frightened voice called , 'What is it, Charles?', 'I'm a desperate man, Lederman. I will kill you without hesitation. Don't attempt to play tricks on me!'

'Oh my God,' the lawyer gasped, 'I . . . what do you want. I've got three children.' His black eyes rolled fearfully. 'Spare me.'

Cautiously Trepper relaxed his grip a little. 'All right, nothing will happen – you'll come to no harm – if you do exactly as I tell you.'

'Anything!'

'Right. Very carefully – remember I'm armed—' Trepper jerked the free hand he had dug deep into his pocket forward threateningly, as if he had a pistol hidden there, 'move back into the flat. I don't want any nosey neighbour listening to what I say to you and informing the flics. Remember, you're a Jew too. They'd not hesitate. With your conk, they'd whip you inside at once.'

'Anything . . . *anything*!' the lawyer gulped.

Slowly, very slowly, the two men moved inside, Trepper kicking the door closed with the back of his foot. Only then did he release the lawyer, to stand facing him and his plump wife, who was biting her thumb in the way women do when they are afraid and puzzled.

'All right now, don't be afraid, I'm not going to harm you,' again he jerked the imaginary pistol in his pocket, 'as long as you do as you are told.'

'What do you want?' the woman managed to stutter, finally.

'Sit down,' Trepper ordered, 'and I'll tell you.'

Gingerly, as if they were lowering themselves onto red-hot coals, the two frightened Jews did as they were commanded. Trepper, although he felt his knees trembling crazily with the effort of forcing himself into the Jewish lawyer's apartment so violently – he wasn't a violent man by nature – made himself remain standing. He felt that position gave him a psychological advantage over the two obviously frightened people staring up at him apprehensively.

Licking dry lips, he began his explanation. 'Now for obvious reasons, you think I am a traitor, Lederman. But it isn't true. I worked for the Boches for reasons which you don't need to know. I escaped from them because I have an urgent mission to carry out which is vital for the success of our cause – *yours and mine*,' he emphasized the words. 'Although you might not agree with my politics, I am after all, a Jew.' He looked pointedly at Lederman, in spite of the fact that he had always been embarrassed by the knowledge he had been born a Jew.

'I see,' Lederman said. 'But everywhere they are saying you are traitor.'

'Possibly,' Trepper answered, in full control of the situation now, thinking on his feet, already seeing in advance the objections the lawyer would make to his next proposal, 'but they don't know the full facts.'

'All right, Trepper, perhaps they don't. But how can I convince Kovalsky and the rest of them that you are not a traitor? The word has gone out from Moscow and you know –' he hesitated for only a fraction of a second –' how slavishly they obey any order from that quarter.'

'Yes, I know all right. But in this particular instance, Moscow simply does not know the full facts. Sometimes the man in the field is better informed than those back in the homeland. 'It's up to you to convince them that I am not a traitor, and that they must help me to find the real traitor. Or don't you believe me, Lederman?'

'Of course, of course, I believe you, Trepper,' the other man gasped hastily, his dark eyes full of fear again. 'But how do I convince *them*? After all, I'm a Zionist – an object of suspicion, although we are serving in a common cause against the Fascists. You know your political friends, they only trust their own kind – the Communists.'

Trepper nodded his agreement. 'I know. But you *must* convince them, Lederman! For if you don't,' he jerked the imaginary pistol in the direction of the lawyer's plump, frightened wife, 'you'd better start looking for another mother for your children . . .'

For forty-eight hours Trepper waited in the tiny flat, cooped up with the lawyer's hysterical wife and the equally frightened children, whom he did not allow to go to school. For forty-eight hours he did not allow himself more than a thirty-minute catnap in the middle of the night, when he could be sure that the woman and the children had finally fallen asleep. For forty-eight hours he did not eat a bite, or drink a drop of water – the ersatz coffee ran out after the first day and he wouldn't allow Madame Lederman out to buy any more – without forcing the woman or her children to taste the food and drink first, just in case she had attempted to poison or drug him. And all those interminable hours of waiting and waiting, not a fifteen-minute period went by without a nervous anxious glance through the window to check whether Lederman had not approached the Gestapo with some deal that would not endanger his own life, yet would surrender him, Trepper, to his hunters.

Just after dawn on the third day of his vigil, Trepper awoke with a start from an uneasy doze. From below there had been the squeal of brakes. He rose hurriedly from the chair in which he had dozed, and rushing to the big French window, carefully drew the black-out curtain to one side.

A *gazogene* was drawn up at the curb below, its engine throbbing noisily. The fact that the car was not driven by a petrol engine meant it didn't belong to the Gestapo. That was a relief. But who were the dark-clothed men now gathering on the pavement below? Suddenly he saw Lederman emerge from the seat next to the driver. Trepper clenched his jaw. The bastard had betrayed him. He had sold him to the Party's strong-arm boys. They were coming up to assassinate him!

Trepper ran hastily across to the dining-room table where he had placed the knife, his only weapon. He gripped it in a hand that trembled badly and posted himself in front of the woman's bedroom. They wouldn't take him that easily, he told himself with grim determination. The woman would go with him.

But when Lederman let himself in, Trepper immediately recognised the man who followed him through the door. It was Kovalsky. He relaxed his grip on the knife, knowing at once that the great Resistance leader would not be party to a cold-blooded murder; that would have been carried out by the CP's goons without his presence.

'You going to carve a joint or something, Trepper?' the Resistance leader asked with a half-smile. 'It's a bit early in the day, isn't it?'

Sheepishly Trepper dropped the knife onto the nearest table. 'I thought it was the Gestapo,' he muttered.

'You're in luck – it isn't.' Kovalsky thrust out his hand. 'Good to see you again, Trepper,' he said, as if he meant it, and then turning to Lederman and the two heavy-set men in leather jackets who had accompanied him up to the flat, ordered, 'Park it, comrades. Take the weight off your big flat feet.'

The two men who, Trepper learned later, were his bodyguard, did as they were commanded, although they kept their hats on and watched the door, as if the Gestapo might come bursting through it at any moment, while Lederman hurried off to reassure himself that his wife and children were all right.

Half-an-hour later, all of them were sitting over glasses of hot rum and water, the only drink in the house, listening attentively while Trepper told his long story – how he had been captured and how finally he had agreed to work the radio game for the Gestapo.

'What else, could I do, Comrade Kovalsky?' he demanded passionately. 'Could I risk the heads of my Orchestra? The Gestapo had them all, first and second violins included. Besides, I forced them to agree not to touch my people who were still at liberty,' he lied glibly. 'It was a very serious decision, involving enormous risks, but I had to take it.'

Kovalsky nodded his head slowly. 'Moscow is very angry with you, you know.'

'I can appreciate that, but I knew sooner or later I would be able to warn the Centre, either by slipping through a false message, or escaping personally, as you see I have done.' He extended his arms to reveal his broad chest, as if he was offering his breast to the death blow if they did not believe him. It was the gesture of an absolutely genuine, honest man.

'Well, you can settle your own account with the Centre in due course,' Kovalsky said, apparently satisfied with Trepper's motives for agreeing to work with the hated Gestapo. 'Now what do you want me to do,'

Trepper's heart leapt. He had pulled it off. But when he spoke, his voice was calm and commanding. 'First, contact Moscow and let them have a true account of what has happened and warn them off from any further contact with the fake Orchestra.'

'It will be done.' Kovalsky said. 'And then?'

'And then, find me that traitor of a pianist of mine.' His big jaw hardened. 'I have an account to settle with that young man ...'

The pianist was bored – bored stiff.

He lay on the hard bed in the convent 'cell', Russian grammar resting unopened on his chest, thinking of women and wishing fervently it was Thursday, when Father D'Arcy, S.J., embarrassed as ever, would escort him to the bought woman. But it was still Tuesday, and there were two days to go before he could enjoy those delightful thirty minutes of paid-for passion.

Now the pianist had spent over six months in the Old Firm's Parisian safe-house, the Convent of the Sisters of St Agonie, a scabrous medieval building situated under the walls of the St. Anne Lunatic Asylum. It was an ideal hiding place, with Mother Superior Sister Henriette and her nine nuns acting as the Old Firm's couriers and messengers for the Paris *Amicol-Reseau*, the SIS's largest circuit in Northern France. But it was a terribly boring place, with nothing for him to do but eat, read the handful of pious books, which was all the Convent possessed, and work at his Russian grammar in preparation for his next assignment. Of course, he knew the Old Firm's reason for not evacuating him back to the U.K., once he had accomplished his mission.

He would be a distinct embarrassment for 'C' if he turned up in London and was recognised by one of the Russian 'eyes' – and they had their 'eyes' everywhere. It wouldn't take the Centre long to put two and two together and come up with five, namely that the Old Firm had been instrumental in betraying an Allied network to the enemy. The fat would certainly be in the fire then. According to *Le Colonel*, the big, bluff, formidable head of 'Amicol', the Old Firm would evacuate him as soon as the invasion of France got underway. In the confusion, his presence in London wouldn't be noted. Besides, as *Le Colonel* had confided to him off the cuff, he probably wouldn't be in the U.K. very long. Why else had 'C' ordered that he should start learning Russian?

The pianist gave a heartfelt sigh, as if he were all of sixty-six, instead of a youthful, very fit twenty-six. What an innocent he had been when he had volunteered for 'special duties' in 1940 to get away from the boredom of a womanless Catterick Camp, where 100,000 young men in peak condition were serviced by a dozen elderly whores in nearby Richmond! He had imagined high adventure, full of action and – hopefully – mysterious, beautiful and, naturally, sexy blondes. Reality had been a let-down. It had been routine and more routine, with long periods of inaction and waiting for something to happen, which often didn't.

Yet, all the same, he knew he was doing more for the country in his present role than if he had stayed in the Army. He was a small piece, a very small one, in an extraordinarily dangerous and intricate game. It was a very British game, played for great odds with the smallest possible stake – a handful of brave men and good brains. Yet its object was of the highest importance: the preservation of the British Empire and of Britain's role as a world leader. And in spite of his flippancy, Wily (if that was really his name) was a product of his time and his class – he was a patriot.

Thus in the narrowness of his poorly heated cell, the pianist opened his Russian grammar with another heartfelt sigh, and wished again that it was Thursday . . .

CHAPTER SIX

Father D'Arcy, S.J., was waiting for him outside the Convent, in the darkened, cobbled Rue de la Sante. They shook hands, and the pianist could feel that the middle-aged Jesuit's palm was damp with sweat. The pianist laughed softly. 'I thought I was the one who was supposed to be excited, Father,' he joked.

Above them the clouds parted and the moon sailed out, as if from a turbulent sea, so that the pianist could see the priest's face. It was agitated, perhaps even afraid. The Englishman was surprised. He knew that Father D'Arcy didn't like this monthly business one bit. Although, as a Jesuit, he had convinced himself – logically, naturally – that a young man like the pianist needed a woman periodically, it offended his moral sense to have to procure a woman for him once a month. Normally he was agitated like this, but it was the first time that the pianist had seen him afraid. 'What's the matter, Father?' he asked, as they set off, striding down the Rue de la Sante towards the Boulevard Arago, where they would take the *metro* before the curfew descended.

'I don't know, my son,' the priest replied. 'They have the usual evening patrols out, that's normal. Yet I have an uneasy feeling.' He cast a scared look over his shoulder, as if he could already hear the hurried, heavy boots of the German 'head-hunters' running after him. There was no one there.

'Do you mean being followed?'

'Yes, something like that.'

The pianist grinned. He was too excited at the thought of the woman soon to come to heed the fears of the middle-aged virginal priest.

'It's a rationalisation on your part, probably, Father. You as a trained Jesuit should know that. Your subconscious – you may call it soul,' he added grandly – 'is rebelling. It is trying to stop you from helping me to commit a sin. Which kind I don't know – grave or mortal, eh?'

The priest ignored the flippancy. He pulled his ankle-length cloak around him more tightly and said through gritted teeth, 'When you've been in this business as long as I have, you can smell these things, that's all. Let's hurry.'

'And where to, this night?' the pianist asked, as they turned into the Boulevard, now almost deserted because of the coldness of the evening and the approach of the curfew.

'Quai d'Orsay.'

The pianist whistled through his front teeth. 'Whew, the Old Firm must be in funds these days. Quai d'Orsay, that's a pretty expensive district. What did she cost you, Father?'

'I prefer not to discuss the subject,' Father D'Arcy said

primly, hurrying towards the *metro* station. 'I find the whole business very unsavoury.'

'But they call it the "pleasures of the flesh",' the pianist said cheerfully, while the pale-faced priest, who had probably never even laid a finger on a woman in the whole of his life, paid for the *metro* tickets.

D'Arcy waited until the usual bored militiaman, accompanied by a helmeted German soldier of the Paris garrison, had checked their ID cards, before he spoke. The carriage was almost empty, save for two cloth-capped working-men sitting up front, staring into nothing. All the same, he whispered, as if there were spies everywhere. 'Now listen, if anything goes wrong, we split up. I'm clean, you're not.'

'Agreed.'

'Don't head for the exit at once. They'll be expecting you to do that. Sneak into the *Egouts* and stick it out there till the – er – heat – is off.' The priest was embarrassed at the use of the word; the pianist could see that. But he decided not to pull his leg about it.

Half-heartedly, his mind full of hot fantasies about the woman, he listened to the priest's explanations of the emergency technique. He was used to the monthly briefing. Whether they went to the whores by bus, on foot, even by cycle-taxi, the priest always had a new emergency technique ready, just in case. The pianist knew it was one of the reasons that the *Amicol Reseau* had survived so long when so many other circuits had disintegrated.

'Now you ask: why the *Egouts*?'

The pianist had not even given the Parisian sewage system a thought, but dutifully he rose to the bait. 'Yes, I had wondered about it.'

D'Arcy nodded sagely, like the teacher he had once been, grateful that the pupil was finally showing some form of interest. 'Because once you are in them, the escape possibilities are manifold. You are not limited to one or two exits, there are probably dozens of them. You see,' he continued, warming to his subject, unaware that the two working-men in the cloth caps at the front of the compartment were lip-reading every word he spoke with ease, following the movements of his lips in his reflection, mirrored in the window in front of them, 'it's not only the sewers that are underneath us now, but also the catacombs, kilometres of them, dating back to the Middle Ages, perhaps even earlier.'

'Is that so,' the pianist exclaimed with feigned interest, while his fantasy occupied itself with the first of the many exotic positions he would ask the whore to take for him.

'Yes, indeed. Do you know that, for instance, in Napoleon's time whole bands of deserters lived down there for years, living off the mushrooms which thrive in the catacombs and sewers?'

The pianist sniffed. 'Not exactly what I would consider a healthy diet,' he muttered.

The priest ignored the comment. 'Now the plan,' he said firmly. 'If we are stopped at any station, straight into the nearest office or lift shaft. You don't take the stairs upwards or the lift in the same direction, you go down. Understood?'

'Understood,' the pianist said in a bored tone. The *metro* was beginning to slow down.

'Why?'

'I don't know and frankly I don't –' The pianist broke off. Up front the two working-men had risen, as if they were preparing to leave the train. But suddenly it flashed through the pianist's brain that there was something strange about them. Why should both of them, ordinary, apparently hard-working artisans, probably coming off the night shift, be carrying the collaborationist newspaper *Je Suis Partout*? *

'Because down there you'll find some sort of entrance to the sewage-catacomb system,' D'Arcy answered his own question. 'Once you're down there, there are manifold possibilities of escape. The Boches can't cover every exit –' He stopped speaking as the train jerked to a halt.

The pianist flung a glance out of the window, all thoughts of the unknown whore vanished now, his body tense and alert, his brain racing. The two men were almost level with the priest and himself. Why were the two of them looking at them so strangely? Why had they their hands hidden beneath the outspread newspapers? Surely they would have stuffed them in their pockets? Outside the platform was empty. No, it wasn't. A familiar figure was standing in the shadows just near the stairs.

As if in a nightmare, where one sees the horror descending upon oneself, but yet one seems unable to move, the pianist remained rooted to his seat, as the two workers dropped their

* I am Everywhere.

newspapers to reveal what they had hidden beneath them. *Automatic pistols*!

'*No!*' D'Arcy's cry of fear shattered the trance.

At that moment, both the workers fired. The priest's cry had unnerved them. Even though they were at such close range, the bullets missed the pianist. At his side the priest started to his feet, and fell the next instant, his chest ripped open by the slugs. The pianist did not wait for the second burst.

Springing to his feet, he kneed the man closest to him. He screamed piteously, and slammed into his comrade, just as he was about to fire again. Together, they tumbled to the blood-slippery floor, next to the dying priest. The door opened with a hiss. The pianist sprang out. At the exit Trepper crouched, half-a-dozen other men standing behind him in the shadows. To his rear, a uniformed man was hurrying from an office, his tunic undone, obviously alarmed by the noise of the firing.

The pianist did not hesitate. He reasoned that Trepper and his goons wouldn't fire in case they hit the *metro* official. He swung round, and started to run towards the man. Behind him he heard Trepper shout, 'After him!'

The official stopped in his tracks. He had a silly pompous face, made more silly and pompous by the thin moustache which adorned his upper lip as if it had been drawn there. 'What in the devil's name is this . . . ?'

The pianist paused only to smash his fist in the official's silly face. He slammed against the wall, screaming shrilly. The pianist ran on. A pistol fired. A slug whined off the tiled wall. The pianist exerted all his strength. He hurtled forward towards the open door. Just as he vanished inside, a burst of fire splintered the length of the door. Wood splinters pattered against his heaving shoulders, as he paused there, chest heaving, staring around, wildly trying to make up his mind what to do next, while the noise of the running feet got louder and louder.

Then he saw the heavy iron door. It must be the one leading below! He grabbed the first catch and jerked at it frantically. It came open with a rusty squeak. The feet were almost there now. He grabbed at the next catch. It wouldn't give! He screamed as the catch tore off his nails. He clawed on, his face contorted with nightmarish fear. He had only a matter of seconds left, before their bullets would be striking the soft flesh of his defenceless back. Abruptly the door opened. Gasping, he heaved. With a rusty squeak the iron door swung open. His nostrils were assailed with the stench of centuries. Then he was clattering and clattering down the winding iron stairs into the evil, pitch-black underworld . . .

CHAPTER SEVEN

The bullet crashed thunderously into the sewer. The flash burst like a scarlet flower. For a brief instant, the nauseating flow of sewage sweeping turgidly through the walls of skulls and bones, piled as high as the cavern's roof, was illuminated by the shot.

'There he is!' Trepper yelled excitedly.

Twenty metres away, the pianist started to run again, sloshing through the ankle-deep, stinking mire, all around him the confusion of pipes and tubes, dripping with the stench and ugly white fungi of centuries. Trepper's men ran after him, flashing their torches to left and right, illuminating their path, sending rats in their hundreds scuttling on soft claws for cover. Twisting and turning desperately, sometimes up to his waist in the foul, evil-smelling mess, the pianist tried to evade them in that dark-green phantasmagoria of the sewers.

But Trepper and his men were not to be thrown off. Convinced that they had him now, and guided by the lights, which he didn't possess, they stumbled and staggered after him, firing as they did so.

Fighting off the choking nausea which threatened to overcome him, the pianist struggled on. Blundering blindly forward in the darkness, slamming into dripping walls, and almost falling into the sickening mess at his feet, he was driven forward by the sure knowledge that if they ever caught him, he would be dead within minutes. But not by a bullet. They would plunge him into the mire and hold him under until all life had been choked out of him. He ran on, gasping frantically for air, his mouth gaping open like an asthmatic about to die.

A slug whined off the wall to his left. In the sudden purple flash and momentary flurry of angry red sparks, he saw that the sewer ran straight ahead for several metres. The pianist's head sank. They couldn't miss now. He plunged on, his shadow thrown ahead of him, gigantically distorted by the light of their torches. Trepper must have realised they had him now, for the pianist heard him cry, 'Aim at his legs . . . Do you hear? *At his legs*! I want the bastard alive!'

Slug after slug howled off the walls on both sides of the

sewer, as he sloshed through the vile goo. The pianist seemed to bear a charmed life. Time and time again, a bullet missed him by centimetres. He stumbled on.

Then tragedy struck. He had almost reached the bend in the sewer when suddenly he stepped into space. He screamed, shrill and hysterical with fear. He was falling. With a hellish splash he was immersed in the drainage pool. '*Look out!*' he heard a frightened, muffled voice call above him, and then the stinking, green-scummed surface closed above his head and he was sinking, sinking, sinking . . .

Trepper ran his torch over the surface of the pool, his chest heaving violently with the effort of the chase. Slowly the ripples were beginning to die away and the green scum was re-forming. The only indication that below its evil-smelling surface there was now a dead body was the battered felt hat the pianist had worn, sailing on the barely agitated surface of the drainage pool.

Behind him one of the Party's killers put away his pistol. He spat into the water. 'Looks, as if that's that, *Grand Chef*,' he said huskily.

'Yes,' Trepper agreed, 'you're right there. But I wonder who the treacherous bastard was really working for?'

The man who had spoken first, shrugged carelessly. 'Well, *Grand Chef*, if you ever make it to heaven –'

'Or to hell,' someone interjected with a dry laugh.

'Or to hell, you'll be able to ask him.'

'Yes, I suppose you're right there, Pierre,' Trepper answered, a little wearily. 'Well, come on, let's get out of here before curfew.'

Slowly and in silence, like a funeral party returning from the cemetery where they had just buried one of their own, they began to plod back the way they had come . . .

EPILOGUE: THE ORCHESTRA LIVES!

'I s . . . suppose you want to s . . . say a sort of last g . . . goodbye, old chap?' the untidy-looking civilian, dressed in his usual sloppy tweed jacket and baggy, unpressed grey flannels, commented in his appalling stutter, as always a faint mocking smile on his pale, boozer's face.

The grey-faced young captain, with a shock of prematurely white hair framing his sombre features, nodded, and stared out morosely at the shabby houses of the Avenue Gabrielle, where the Old Firm had set up its Parisian headquarters immediately after the Liberation.

'You're n . . . not exactly a great c . . . conversationalist, old chap,' stuttered the senior SIS man, who would soon be his new chief in the top-secret anti-Russian op.

The young captain merely grunted. His companion gave in. He settled himself more comfortably into the staff car's hard seat. He, too, concentrated on the shabby face of a January Paris, burdened down with heavy snow, worn out by six years of war and now confronted by the threat of a new German occupation, if the Allies didn't manage to stop Rundstedt's surprise offensive through the snow-bound Belgian Ardennes.

The capital was virtually empty of Allied troops – even the base wallahs had been rushed up to the Front to bolster up the crumbling line. The only military traffic was the line of camouflaged American trucks, driven by yellow-eyed, frozen Negroes, which barred the staff car's progress to Orly for nearly ten minutes.

'Red B . . . Ball Express,' the shabby civilian explained, as the staff-car driver gunned his engine impatiently. 'All the way from the beaches to the F . . . Front. No-one has the right to stop the –'

At that moment the driver saw a gap in the steady line of trucks. He shot forward. The nearest truck driver braked hastily, and the captain caught a glimpse of an angry, frightened coal-black face under a too-small helmet. 'Al . . . almost no-one,' the civilian stuttered, taking a deep breath of relief. 'But I don't r . . . recommend you do that again, driver. Those b . . . black drivers k . . . know no mercy.'

'Bloody darkies!' the driver grunted.

Next to the civilian the captain did not even seem to notice the incident; apparently he was preoccupied with his own thoughts, whatever they might be.

The rest of their journey through Paris to Orly Field was

without incident. At the gate the heavily armed 'Snowdrops'*, as the Parisians called the American MP's, approached the staff car cautiously. There were German saboteurs everywhere this January, many dressed in Allied uniform, and they were taking no chances. But the civilian's special pass soon disarmed their suspicions. They were passed through the gate with a flourish and started to roll towards one of the two runways still operational after the recent German air raid.

'N . . . nice salute, for a . . . Yank,' the civilian stuttered, unable to restrain that latent anti-Americanism of his, which his companion had already noted went deeper with him than was customary in high-ranking Old Firm circles. But he didn't comment on it. His gaze was now fixed on the C-47, decorated with the red star of the Soviet Union, drawn up on the nearest of the two runways, its twin engines already beginning to warm up for the long flight to Moscow.

The civilian ordered the driver to pull up behind the American Air Transport Command's wooden barracks HQ 'S . . . safer there, old chap,' he explained to his companion. 'Can s . . . see, without b . . . being seen, what?'

The Captain nodded, running his hard blue eyes along the length of the American lease-lend machine. Apparently the passengers had not yet taken their places, for he could not see them.

'S . . . Stalin's personal plane,' the civilian was saying. 'Uncle Joe lent it to Maurice Thorez† to bring the old boy back to *La Belle France*. S'pect they're g . . . going to have a c . . . crack at Charlie de Gaulle.'

The captain nodded absently, his eyes still searching the plane's narrow round windows for that well-remembered face. Suddenly he saw him. There was no mistaking that broad, pale, yet still confident face under the cropped wavy hair. It was him all right.

The captain's mind flashed back to that terrible night, eighteen months before, when he had last seen that face. That drainage pool had been a blessing in disguise after all. Gasping, spluttering, choking, he had fallen and fallen, wondering when he would ever hit the bottom and be granted the mercy of a quick death. But he was not to die – not just then.

* On account of their white-painted helmets.

† Head of the French Communist Party, who had been in Russia for the previous four years.

Suddenly he found himself sprawled on his back in shallow water, completely winded, his arm broken by the fall, and every bone in his body screaming out with the agony of the impact. It had taken him an age to stagger to his feet. But he knew he had to move on, knowing that the heavy lassitude which threatened to overcome him came from the sewer gas. If he stayed there long, it would kill him. He would die alone in the rat-filled darkness, deep below the surface of Paris.

Stark, blind, atavistic fear had forced him on, stumbling, shambling, down endless foul-smelling corridors, alive with scampering rats. *He must find an exit!*

He had forgotten his pursuers. They had belonged to another, remoter world. His sole concern was to get out of this nightmarish world of dark, dank, dripping desolation. After a while he had begun to scream, the screams trailing after him down the endless sewers, sending the myriad rats scampering away in green-eyed panic. But when he had almost given up hope, his crazed progress had come to a shocked halt. He had run into a blank wall! He couldn't go on any further. For what must have been a long time, he had remained there sunk to his knees in despair, sobbing like a frightened child, until finally he had become aware of the current of cooler air playing about his bent head. Slowly, very slowly, he had looked up.

High above his head he could just make out a faint circle of light. His heart had leapt with joy. It was a manhole cover! He knew it instantly. '*Manhole cover,*' he had babbled to himself crazily, '*way out . . . out . . .*'

How he had managed to scramble up the wall with his broken arm, he could never understand later. Nor how he had managed to raise the hatch. For it had been jammed. He had strained and heaved and pushed until he thought he must burst a blood vessel. But in the end it had given, and he had lain there, half in, half out of the hole, greedily drinking in the crystal air, revelling in its headiness. He had been reprieved . . .

'W . . . well, old chap, it looks as if the conductor is on his way to the W . . .Workers' Paradise,' the civilian broke into his reverie, raising his voice over the sudden roar of the C-47's twin engines. 'Wonder if they've got a new Orchestra lined up for him!'

The captain licked suddenly dry lips, and rolling down the window, poked out his head to get a last look at the man who had controlled his destiny for so long in that strange three-sided battle in the shadows of these last years. Something made Trepper turn. Just as the scarlet flame spurted from the exhausts, his startled eyes saw the captain and his mouth dropped foolishly, as his lips formed the silent words '*The pianist!*'

A moment later the plane commenced rolling forward, gathering speed at every instant. The face became a pale blur and then vanished altogether as the plane shuddered, bounced once, twice, on the rough ground, and was abruptly airborne, its lights winking like fireflies as it ascended higher and higher into the grey winter sky. Within minutes it had vanished into the long range of coldly corrugated clouds, heading steadily towards the east and another world.

'C . . . come on,' the civilian urged. 'It's b . . . bloody cold here with that window open. Let's t . . . tuck ourselves round a big double brandy. That's the last you'll ever see of that particular m . . . musician.'

Slowly the captain turned to look at the civilian. The man had said the words with certainty of prior knowledge. But the civilian's face revealed nothing; it was as mocking and as cynical as ever.

'Yes, I suppose you're right, Philby,' he whispered and rolled down the window dutifully.

The car pulled away, leaving the field empty and desolate behind them . . .

It is recorded that the *Grand Chef*, Leopold Trepper, arrived back in Moscow, after a long plane ride via Cairo, Teheran and Baku, on the morning of January 14th, 1945. It was six years since he had last been in Moscow and he set off to visit the Centre in the capital's Znamensky Street with an undisguised feeling of pride at his achievements during that long period in the underground. On arrival he was shown into the Director's office immediately. The conversation between the two spymasters was brief and bitter.

The Director asked: 'What are your plans for the future?'

'Before talking about the future,' Trepper retorted hotly, 'we might have a word about the past! Why didn't you believe me from the beginning? How were you able to mess up things so miserably? I sent you enough warnings, didn't I?'

The Director remained unmoved. 'Have you returned simply to settle accounts?' he asked coldly.

'And why not?'

'In that case,' the Director replied, 'they won't be settled in my office.' He pressed the bell on his big desk. Two six-foot officers in uniform appeared. They seized the *Grand Chef* by both arms and marched him out to the waiting car, its windows covered by curtains. With its siren howling to clear the snow-bound Moscow streets, Trepper was driven straight to the feared Lubianka Prison. He was to remain there for the next ten years. He was no longer needed. The Centre had a new Orchestra and a new conductor . . .

It is also recorded that one month after the *Grand Chef* began his long sentence in solitary confinement, willing himself to survive the 'gang' (as he called them to his cellmates), who had betrayed him after such long service to the Communist cause, Captain Wily – if that was really his name – was found dead, just before dawn, in the middle of a blacked-out Avenue Gabrielle.

His head was crushed beyond recognition (they identified him by his Army pay-book) and his chest was crushed to pulp, as if several heavy vehicles had passed over him in the darkness after he had been first knocked down. In the end, the French police – and the MI5 men who had been rushed from London to conduct a private inquiry – concluded that Wily had been knocked over by a Red Ball Express truck on its way to the front, and that following trucks had passed over the unconscious agent until all life had been crushed out of him. Undoubtedly, so the police and the security men told themselves, it had been a slow and very painful death.

Philby, Wily's late chief, made an approach to General Bull, who was in charge of COMZ*. Bull made some tentative inquiries in an attempt to find the driver or drivers concerned. But nothing much came of them. The Allied armies were preparing for the great assault on the Rhine, and Bull confided privately to the stuttering, shabby representative of the 'Old Firm', 'Shoot, those niggers o' mine can see only the Front and them Frog whores waitin' for them back at Base. They sure drive like crazy!' That had been that. On the day that the great assault commenced, which would bring the final downfall of the Thousand-Year Reich and which the white-haired pianist had not lived to see, the inquiry into his death was closed.

Back in London, the new conductor passed the signal to the Russian pianist to encode. 'S . . . see it goes t . . . today, old chap,' he said in his appalling stutter, and grinned, obviously

* U.S. rear-line troops.

very pleased with himself that everything in Paris had gone off so smoothly.

Two hours later, the music box began to play and the signal was on its way. It was short and simple and meant nothing to anyone in Moscow save the Director at the Centre. It read: 'Mission carried out as ordered. Pianist fired.'

The new orchestra had commenced its first concert . . .